TAKE THE KIDS
FISHING
THEY'RE BETTER THAN
WORMS

Roger Pond

Other Books by Roger Pond

It's Hard To Look Cool When Your Car's Full Of Sheep
Tales From The Back Forty
(Humor)

Things that go "Baa!" in the Night
Tales from a Country Kid
(Humor)

My Dog Was A Redneck But We Got Him Fixed
Tales From The Back Forty
(Humor)

The Livestock Showman's Handbook:
A Guide to Raising Animals for Junior Livestock Shows
(Informational)

TAKE THE KIDS FISHING THEY'RE BETTER THAN WORMS

Tales from a Country Kid

ROGER POND

Pine Forest Publishing

Copyright © 2001, by Roger Pond
All Rights Reserved

First Printing, October 2001
Second Printing, November 2007

Library of Congress Control # 2001 130783

Publishers Cataloging-in-Publication Data

Pond, Roger, 1944-
Take The Kids Fishing, They're Better Than Worms
1. Humor
I. Title

ISBN # 0-9617766-5-X

Published by Pine Forest Publishing
314 Pine Forest Road
Goldendale, Washington 98620

Cover by Mark Mohr

Printed in the United States of America

To Hannah and Henry,
whose fishing stories remain to be told.

TABLE OF CONTENTS

ACKNOWLEDGMENTS

These stories have appeared in newspapers throughout the United States and Canada that use *The Back Forty* column. I am grateful to publishers and editors who have found in their hearts and their budgets to use the column these many years.

I am also grateful to Mark Mohr for his artistic talent in cover design and to Carol York and Pete Fotheringham of Gorge Publishing for expert design assistance and electronic page layout.

A special thanks to my wife, Connie, for tolerating all of those stories that may have been stretched slightly.

• • • • • **PLEASE NOTE** • • • • •

This book contains fictitious names. Any resemblance of
these names to those of people you may know is purely
coincidental. These stories are not to be taken seriously.

Take The Kids Fishing,
They're Better Than Worms

"Be careful," my wife said as I left the house. "Your life insurance isn't very good."

"We'll be careful alright," I told her. That's what I always say at 4:00 A.M. I never go hunting or fishing with the idea of doing anything stupid.

This morning was different, I guess. "We're going in with the flashlights, huh?" I asked my son. "Where is the trail, anyway?"

"Just follow me," he said. "I think we cross the creek down there somewhere."

I pointed my flashlight at the creek and noticed it was a roaring chute of rocks and waterfalls. Russ jumped on a rock in the middle, then across to the other side.

I thought back to the days when my son was small, and I carried him across creeks on my back. When he got bigger I inspired him by saying, "If you cross right here, I think you can make it."

I looked at this natural version of a waterslide and wondered if Russ might come back and carry me across? That didn't seem likely, but he was full of encouragement.

"If you jump to that rock and then this one, I think you can make it," he said.

Times like these invoke life's most basic questions. "Is it better to jump on a wet rock with a dry boot, or a dry rock with a wet boot? What if I miss? How many bones are there in a person's body, anyway?"

I chose the dry rock with a wet boot — and made it. Then, we headed up a ridge and around a series of cliffs on a trail made by a family of chipmunks.

"This boy is trying to kill me!" I thought. "Nah, he wouldn't do that. I've got his fishing rod."

Finally, we got to the river. "Here are some corkies, and beads, and some leaders," Russell said.

"The yarn is in there, and the weights are in my pack. The bead goes on first, then the corkie. I tied-up some droppers in this pocket here," he instructed.

"Well, isn't this nice?" I thought. "After all these years of Russ borrowing my stuff, now I'm using his rod, his bait, and his fishing gear. He's even tying the knots for me!"

I remembered when my son first started fishing. He was just big enough to sit on a log and probably didn't jump across creeks any better than I do today.

I loaned him a rod and tied on his hooks. I even gave advice on the best places to fish — and did most of his casting at first.

Now, he teaches me how to fish and loans me stuff I didn't even know I needed. Funny how things change.

"Here, Dad, let me show you how to do that," he said. "You've got to make more loops or the knots won't hold.

"Cast over there in that back eddy. Keep your bait on the bottom — and don't move it around so much.

"Here, give me that. I'll show you how to cast with one of these reels."

Let The Cat Get It

I don't know what causes it, but there's something about sales calls that drives me crazy. The calls themselves don't bother me so much, but I'm always embarrassed by the answers I give them.

Last week Jennifer called to say, "I'm calling to tell you about our new voice messaging service you can receive free for the next 30 days. Do you understand how our voice messaging service will help you with your calls?"

"I think so, but we don't want to do it," I said.

"How do you handle your calls when you are away from the phone?" she asked quickly.

"We have several ways," I told her. "Thanks for calling. Bye."

"I think so, but we don't want to do it?" "We have several ways?" What a dumb set of answers.

You would think a person who has been through high school, college, numerous county fairs, and a couple of goat ropings could come up with something better than that!

Every time I get one of those calls, I hang up thinking,

"Why did I say that?" My goal is to get rid of them quickly. Still, "We have several ways" is a darned poor response.

There are a million things a person could say when someone asks if we understand their new phone service. We might say, "Duh? I dunno. Maybe you should send me a letter or somethin'."

Better yet, I could state, "Thank you for calling Roger Pond. This is his bleeping message machine. Please leave your name and number after the bleep. Blee-e-e-p!

"If you would like to speak to a real person, you could hang on the line until one happens by. Or you may wish to call another number and see who you get. Blee-e-e-p!"

When Jennifer asks how I handle calls when I'm away from the phone, I could say, "What? You mean people call me when I'm not here?!"

I should have told her, "I let the dog get the phone when I'm away." Or, "Our cat loves messages. You want to talk to her?"

How about, "If it weren't for folks like you, we wouldn't have to answer the phone so often."

But instead I say something like, "We have several ways."

I'll be ready next time, though. Next time AT&T or MCI calls I'll be prepared for them, too. I'm making a list.

When they mention their "friends and family" program I'll tell them, "I don't have any friends, and my family won't talk to me."

If they offer me $100 to switch companies, I'll say, "I can't take money from strangers." When they ask how many phones we have, I'll say, "I don't know. I only use one at a time."

Uh-oh, the phone's ringing! It's them! I know it's them. Where's my list? Where's the %$#@ list?

Maybe I'll just let the cat get it.

A Fine Mess

"Well, isn't this a fine mess?" I mumbled. "Just a few more and I'll have enough for breakfast."

That may sound strange to some folks, but mushroom hunters will understand. Getting one's self into a fine mess is about the best thing that can happen to a mushroom hunter.

I grew up in the Midwest in the days when mushroom hunting was a heady blend of art, science, and religion. There was a certain mythology to mushroom hunting when I was a kid.

We always looked around apple trees, for example; and oak groves were good — as were beech, ash, hickory, maple, gum, sycamore, poplars, walnut, hawthorn, hedge apples, etc. We always looked in the mayapple patches. We found the vast majority of our mushrooms in the places we always looked.

Dedicated hunters carried a stick and raked the leaves to uncover the secretive morels. Some dragged their feet as they walked, hoping to cover their tracks so no one would find their mushroom patch.

That's part of the lore of mushroom hunting: You never know where you'll find them, but you surely aren't going to tell anybody else where you've been looking.

I've learned to choose my mushroom hunting companions carefully. I'll never take a person who has never found a mushroom, for example. There's a reason they've never found a mushroom, and there's no point in dragging a jinx through the woods with you.

I get a kick out of those old stories about blindfolding your companions before taking them mushroom hunting. That's a bunch of baloney. Ninety percent of them will try to peak under the blindfold as soon as they get in the car.

Some of my best mushroom hunts started out as something else. We would be planting corn and park the fertilizer truck next to a woods, or we might find some mushrooms at the edge of a lane.

Those were the days when portable outhouses were unheard of, but every farm had a woodlot. If a guy was working in the field he always spent part of his day in the woods.

It's hard to say how many mushrooms are found by folks who are actually looking for a paw-paw tree, but we found quite a few that way.

My favorite mushroom hunt started out as a turkey hunt. I was wandering around waiting for a turkey to gobble, when I happened to spot a few morels. The turkeys weren't cooperating anyway, so I put the mushrooms in my hat.

A few minutes later I found some more — and my hat was getting full. So I took off my T-shirt and tied the top shut.

By the time my T-shirt was full the turkey hunt had escalated into a full-blown mushroom hunt. Finally, I didn't have any place to put them.

So I took off my long underwear and tied the legs shut. A few hours later my underwear was fully loaded, and I took that as a sign it was time to quit.

Some folks might wince at carrying mushrooms around in their underwear, but that's because they aren't mushroom hunters. We can't expect them to understand, now can we?

Orange Shoes

The sport of fishing has certainly changed over the years. I can remember when a well-stocked tackle box contained a few Lazy Ikes and a package of rubber worms.

Today's well-heeled fisherman has more equipment than he can ever use and a complete wardrobe to go along with it. We've come a long way from the days when we fished with what we had and wore whatever we could find.

That's the way it was when my cousin, Dean, made his ill-fated fishing trip back in the 60's. Dean was just out of college and recently married. He didn't have a lot of money for fishing equipment or clothes.

He found some rods and lures, but the only fishing shoes he could find were an old pair his dad bought many years before. The old shoes were comfortable enough, but they had one small flaw: They were bright, shiny orange.

"Who cares?" Dean thought. "We're just going fishing." So he and his buddy, Jim, loaded up the car and headed for Dale Hollow Reservoir.

To make a long story short, the two young fellows caught

nothing in three days of hard fishing, while an old guy down the way returned to the dock each noon with a nice stringer of fish.

Finally, Dean couldn't stand it any longer. He laced up his shoes and walked over to talk with the old fisherman.

The old-timer wasn't very friendly, but Dean is pretty good at breaking the ice with strangers. "That's a nice stringer of fish you've got there," he said. "If a couple of guys like my buddy and I wanted to duplicate the good fishing you've been having, what would you suggest we use?"

The old guy stared at the ground a few seconds and said dryly, "If I was you, I think I'd just use them orange shoes."

This didn't improve the young men's trip, and they headed for home a couple of days later. My cousin and his buddy were barely on the road before Dean needed a restroom.

"No problem," Jim said. "I need some gas, anyway. We'll stop at the next station."

They finally found a gas station, and Dean ran for the restroom. He headed for the first stall he could find.

Cousin Dean was just thinking what a nice place this was, when he looked down and saw a blue skirt rustling in the stall beside him. "Oh, no! I'm in the wrong restroom!" he thought.

He headed for the door at the first opportunity and ran back to the car. "Have you paid for the gas yet?" he asked his buddy.

"Not yet," Jim said. "Why?"

"Let's get out of here," Dean said. The two young men handed the attendant a ten dollar bill and jumped in their car.

As they pointed their car toward the freeway, a woman's voice rang out from inside the station. "AND HE WAS WEARING ORANGE SHOES!" she screamed

School Reform

Everyone's talking about school reform. We're told schools need more money, better teachers, new programs, more computers, and modern technology if our students are to succeed in the coming millennium.

Where will we get the money? From the federal government, I presume.

Readers of my generation might remember when kids learned more with less money, worse teachers, old programs, and no computers. How can that be?

Maybe the kids have something to do with it? (What the heck is a millennium, anyway?)

I'm certainly not against school funding. I just hate to see it come from the federal government.

So much of that money gets diverted. Every year someone orders a new shipment of commodes, cleverly disguised as television sets.

School reform and "social promotion" have become political buzzwords recently. Nobody heard of those things when I was a kid.

My teachers talked about reform school, but they never mentioned school reform. Social promotion was just another expression for teaching the boys how to dance. Don't get me wrong about social promotion. I suspect it has a place in certain instances, despite the political posturing we've been hearing recently.

I'll bet some of my old teachers would admit to bending a grade once in awhile. You can't blame them really. Every year somebody had to call the janitor to get some kid untangled from his seat.

"For gosh sakes!" the janitor would say. "This boy is getting too big for this seat. All he needs is a couple of D's!"

Schools have seen a number of reforms over the years. Most of them have gone around two or three times.

I went to school when "tracking" and "ability grouping" were the big thing. The idea of college prep was relatively new.

We didn't have to take foreign languages like the college prep kids do today. Universities figured, "What good are all these languages if the students don't know where the countries are anyway?"

So I enrolled in vocational agriculture. That put me on the "vocational track." I planned to go to college, but our principal figured, "Tracking is tracking, and a person needs to make up his mind."

Each year he would look at my vocational agriculture major and place me in some classes he reserved for the victims of social promotion. I would look around and wonder, "Wow, I must have flunked that last test worse than I thought."

I can remember my English teacher asking, "Roger, how did you get in this class?"

"Gosh, I don't know," I told her. "The principal and I haven't been hitting it off too good lately."

Watch Out For The Green Weenie

"Haruum-voom," the Toyota droned as I shifted into third; "Voom—voom," when I dropped back into second.

"My big, powerful SUV seems to be having a little trouble with this hill," I quipped to my companions. "You would think a monster four-cylinder like this would roar right up this little grade."

That's what I've been reading in the newspapers. Sports utility vehicles are supposed to be gas-guzzling monsters, capable of blowing other vehicles off the road.

So how did I get a dinky four-cylinder, barely able to pull a large piece of taffy? Other SUV owners may be wondering the same thing. Any car that can run over a baseball without crashing has suddenly become a gas-guzzling monster.

Here's a feature from the New York Times News Service with the headline, "Automakers Plan Less Deadly SUVs." The story is prefaced with, "Finally admitting the behemoths can be hazardous, companies are tweaking designs to protect motorists in crashes."

A more accurate appraisal might be, "SUVs are safe. Other cars are dangerous."

The problem is SUVs are taller and heavier than other cars on the average. They do more damage in a crash with a smaller car.

Liberal thinkers say that's not fair. Someone should level the playing field by putting more plastic into SUVs and lowering them to the approximate height of an armadillo.

What a bunch of baloney! Nobody ever worried about our '55 Chevys, '57 Fords, or the venerable Thunderbird being out of sync with other cars on the road. We made them any height we wanted; and they were heavy enough they weren't going to get run over by a minivan.

The '54 Chevy I drove to college was probably heavier than my modern SUV, and she could take a hit with the best of them. The "Green Weenie," as my friends called her, wasn't about to get flattened by some wild-eyed fiend in a Jeep.

The Weenie was big enough to take care of herself, and she had that special transmission they called "Power Glide." The old Chevy could go from 0 to 60 in a matter of minutes. Getting back to 0 took a bit longer.

That's what happened when my fraternity brother, Dave, borrowed the Green Weenie for a trip to campus. Dave was barely out of the fraternity house parking lot when a kid in a Corvette came flying out of a side street and hit him broadside.

The 'Vette was stopped at the intersection, but the driver didn't see Dave coming. Or, if he did, he probably thought the Weenie was stationary.

Whatever he thought, the kid floored his Corvette and hit Dave right in the driver's side door. The good news is nobody was hurt. A dent in the door was the extent of damage to my old Chevy.

The 'Vette was fiberglass, though. It was nearly totaled.

That was a lesson for me. I've never wanted a sports car, and I'm not real fond of fiberglass; but I don't care what other folks drive.

I figure we should drive what works for us. Drivers just need to slow down a little — and watch out for the Green Weenie.

It's An Antique

I guess I'll never be a collector of antiques. There's something about buying stuff someone else threw away that seems backwards to me.

Even though I don't understand antiques, I enjoy watching "Antiques Roadshow" on public television. Folks who haven't seen the show will have to bear with me — it's like a huge flea market where the guests bring their antiques to have them appraised.

A commentator says, "Tell me a little more about this watch, Hazel. You say it belonged to your grandfather who worked for the railroad."

"Yes, Grandpa Casey used to ride the trains back in Tennessee," Hazel explains. "He used this watch to tell how far it was to the next town, and how long it would be until lunch time. Grandma said if it weren't for his watch, Grandpa would have starved to death."

"When we look at the back of the watch we see it was made in Kentucky around the turn of the century," the commentator explains. "Many of these time pieces were made by elves who lived in the forests.

"Your Grandpa may have gotten the watch from an elf who was riding the train. That was pretty common in those days, because the elves weren't very big."

"I think this watch at auction would be worth around $12,000 today. If you still had the elf, it would be worth considerably more. Does that surprise you?"

"Oh my, yes!" Hazel says. "That's a lot of money, but I would never consider selling it, of course."

That's what gets me about the antiques people. They want to know what it's worth, but they would never consider selling it!?

Who cares what it's worth if you aren't going to sell it? By the same token, who knows what it's worth if you can't sell it?

The Antiques Roadshow always reminds me of the stuff I keep out in the barn. I wonder how my grandkids would explain my collection of useful items?

A commentator asks, "Well, Hannah, I see you have some old fishing equipment here. You say this belonged to your grandfather?"

"Yes. We have nearly everything Grandpa ever owned. Grandma always said he had a bit of a cheap streak in him."

"I can see the first object is an old, rusty tackle box, with a few railroad spikes in the bottom," the commentator says. "The other one has me puzzled, though. Your Grandpa called it a drift sack?"

"That's what he called it. He would tie it to the back of his boat when the wind was blowing," Hannah explains.

"I believe the term 'drift sack' may be a play on words," the commentator suggests. "This looks like an old feed sack your Grandpa reconstructed to avoid buying a drift sock!

"Apparently he sewed a piece of garden hose into the neck of the sack and tied the whole shebang to the back of his boat. Do you have any idea what this is worth!?"

"I have no idea," Hannah says. "But it doesn't matter. I'd never consider selling it, anyway."

Looking Cool

It's hard to look cool when your car's full of sheep. But looking cool isn't everything, as a recent item from the London Times illustrates. The story originated in Scotland and was snatched from the internet by a couple of Brits (English Brits) at the University of Illinois.

These folks have one of my books, *It's Hard To Look Cool When Your Car's Full Of Sheep*, and wanted me to know I'm not the only one who hauls sheep in his car. I think they also wanted to show how far the Scots might go with a buck or two — pardon the pun.

It seems the ferry company, Caledonian MacBayne, got softhearted last spring and lowered their fares for crofters (Scottish farmers) on the islands of Uist, Barra, Mull, and Colonsay. These farmers were taking livestock to market on the mainland at great expense, and Caledonian MacBayne decided to give them a break by charging only for the livestock and waving the vehicle fee.

It costs more than 100 pounds ($170) for islanders to take a vehicle to the mainland, so the new fares were quite a break for farmers with just a few head to sell. Sheep cost 2.35 pounds per head, for example.

Within a few weeks the ferry staff knew something was up. A car full of suitcases would come through with one or two sheep in the back. The driver paid for the sheep and the rest went free.

A fortnight later the same car and passengers would return with the animals and a grim story about the market for sheep on the mainland. "Auch mon! I couldn't let her go for such a pittance."

Soon more cars were arriving with a sheep or two in the back. And the sheep looked so comfortable. Some of them probably had their own suitcases.

Reports have it the crofters were leaving their woollys with a cooperative farmer on the mainland and heading off on vacation before picking up the sheep for the return trip. Why didn't these folks sell the sheep so they wouldn't have to haul them back?

I can answer that one. It takes too long to potty train one of those things to just unload it for market price.

Even then the ferry folks couldn't believe a Scotsman would do such a thing. Finally, one ferryman said to another, "I don't think I've seen that farmer before, but the sheep looks very familiar."

This went on throughout the summer until one day the ferry staff decided to expose this scam once and for all.

A large, burly fellow was returning with a sheep in the front seat of his car, when the ferryman asked, "I thought you were taking that sheep to the auction on the mainland?"

"Oh, I took her there yesterday," the Scotsman said. "And we had so much fun that today I'm taking her to the gallery downtown."

(That's the essence of the Times story — except for the last few paragraphs and some dialog I manufactured to flesh it out a bit. They can't shoot a guy for that, can they?)

How To Cook A Groundhog

Hunting seasons are a time of excitement for many — and a source of confusion for others. Non-hunters must wonder why folks enjoy getting up in the middle of the night, stumbling around looking for a baloney sandwich, and sitting on a cold rock for days at a time.

I don't understand it, either; so I'm not going to try to explain it to others. Maybe it's the thrill of the chase?

Not everyone is thrilled, of course. And quite a few wives are less than ecstatic when the old man drags something home for dinner.

I can sympathize with the wives, but the folks who really deserve our empathy are those who work in sporting goods stores. They listen to the tall tales of fishermen all summer, and then in the fall, they get another dose of preposterous yarns from hunters.

I stopped by our local sporting goods store last week to inquire about a "big buck contest" they used to sponsor. I learned the contest was discontinued years ago.

"Oh, we don't do that anymore," the clerk said. "And I

am so happy not to have to look at those hairy faces with their glazed-over eyes and tongues hanging out while I measure a deer's antlers."

That's just the hunters. She said some of the deer were pretty ugly, too.

I learned years ago the sight of wild game doesn't appeal to everyone. Friends and family must be conditioned to the sight and taste of game, much as a puppy is introduced to the sound of gunfire.

I was married only a few short weeks when I bagged my first groundhog for dinner. I have hunted woodchucks since I was 12, but never thought about eating one before that fateful day.

My brother, Kenny, convinced me groundhogs are good to eat when they are about half grown. So I happened to find one that was just the right size and took it home for dinner.

My young bride saw me finishing the cleaning job, and said, "Oh, you shouldn't have done that. They're not in season, are they?"

That's when I realized Connie thought I had bagged a rabbit. This was a long way from rabbit season, and breaking game laws is pretty much out of character for me; but I thought, "Hey, is it better for my new wife to think I shot a rabbit out of season, or to realize I am about to cook a groundhog?"

That's what I thought, too. There's no sense in muddying the water for a person who likes rabbit, but probably wouldn't eat a groundhog if it was cooked by Julia Child.

So I browned it in a skillet and baked it in the oven until I thought it was done. Then, I baked it some more to be sure it was done. It wasn't bad, but it wasn't good, either.

What does all this have to do with hunting — or with folks who work in sporting goods stores? I don't know, but it gives us a pretty good idea of the crazy stories those people have to listen to.

Free Range Chicken

Everyone has their own ideas about sales. Most of us have a negative image of salespeople — except for the ones we know personally. Then we like them just fine.

I recently read a column by a man who gives sales seminars. At one session this fellow asked folks in the audience, "How many of you didn't like salespeople before you got into sales?"

Nearly everyone raised their hands. Then he asked his audience, "Now that you are a salesperson yourself, how many of you still don't like salespeople?"

Almost everyone raised their hands again! This fellow says this just proves salespeople should do their best not to act like salespeople.

Much of the negative image accorded to salespeople comes from those who travel door to door. I always get a kick out these folks and their little tricks.

I remember back in the late '70's when one company sent a very attractive young woman around the country to sell their fertilizer. Some of our local farmers had record crops that year. They finally bought enough fertilizer.

Just recently we had a fellow stop by to sell us some

frozen food. He and my wife were standing in front of his truck talking when I got home from fishing, and I could tell he was not happy to see me.

This was a Saturday, so I hadn't shaved, and I don't dress very well when I go fishing. I may have looked a little rough around the edges.

"Come over here and look at this food," my wife said. "We were talking about getting some frozen chicken, and this man can sell us a combination of chicken and seafood for $74."

"This is a special offer just for today," the sales guy said. "I'm not supposed to do this, but I can give you two of these boxes for $148 or I can split them into one box for just $74."

"Seventy-four dollars!?" I exclaimed. "How much does a box weigh?"

"Our company doesn't go by weight," he said. "We go by servings. There are 54 servings in a box."

"Fifty-four servings for a canary!" I thought to myself.

The salesman waved a chicken breast in front of my nose and said, "This is all organic, free-range chicken. There are absolutely no chemicals in it."

"I won't eat anything that doesn't have chemicals in it," I said flatly.

The salesman tried to laugh, but I could see it wasn't easy for him.

"Do you have a price list you can leave with us?" I asked.

"We don't do price lists. This is a special offer," he growled — as he folded up his boxes and headed for the back of his truck.

I walked back toward my boat and overheard the salesman mumble something about spending $100 for gasoline to go buy our groceries. I should have gone back and told him how far the modern automobile will go on $100 worth of gasoline.

I could have said, "I buy gas by the gallon, but my car uses very small servings."

I let him go, though. He looked like he'd had enough.

Hang On To Your Bags

It's easy to forget how much air travel has changed over the years. I remember the days when a person could walk into an airport, hand over his suitcase, and get on the plane.

Now, we arrive hours before takeoff, park the car miles away, and spend half the morning answering questions about how our bags were packed. Then we jump on a conveyer and ride through the airport — just like a bale of hay entering the barn.

Someday I'm going to tell the baggage clerk, "No, I didn't pack my bag. My wife packed it. And neither you, nor I are supposed to know what's in it."

All of this hassle comes in the name of progress and security. I can't speak for everyone, but I felt better in the old days — when I could see where my baggage went.

The concept of airline "hubs" with huge planes and enormous airports has gone too far in my opinion. We're getting to the point where it costs more to park the car than it does to buy the plane ticket.

Why can't the airlines help upgrade the smaller airports

where a person could find his way around, instead of building a monstrosity no one can even get into?

I have fond memories of flying into the little airport at Pendleton, Oregon — many years ago when United Airlines still scheduled flights there. The Pendleton Airport was small then, and I don't suppose it's any bigger now that United has abandoned the premises.

I sat in that airport one morning and watched the wind howling down the runway. You can't see the wind in many parts of the country, but you can in Pendleton. The wind there is full of things: Russian thistles, Jim Hill Mustard, pieces of driftwood.

This particular morning, windows rattled and lights in the airport lobby began to flicker. I wondered if this was a normal day for that part of the country.

A woman staggered in from the parking lot to report someone tried to open the hood on his car. The wind peeled the hood back like someone opening a new can of Spam. "Must have been a tourist," the woman surmised.

Soon after that a fifty-gallon oil drum went rolling across the runway. I figured the breeze was freshening.

Airport personnel suggested it was probably an empty oil drum I saw. "The planes don't fly when full ones are blowing."

I handed my suitcase to a luggage clerk, and he handed it to the guy behind him. I don't know what that fellow did with it.

I wasn't worried, though. It's pretty hard to lose your luggage when there's only one airplane.

The baggage clerk was the same person who took my ticket and ushered me onto the plane. I think he was in charge of security, too, judging from the little badge on his shirt. Those were the days before metal detectors, photo I.D.s, and $8 per day parking.

Some folks might like the big modern airports, but I don't. If I had my druthers, I'd still be flying out of Pendleton.

Road Hog

I guess I'll never understand economics. Each time there's a freeze in Florida the price of citrus spikes up a few notches.

But when the hog market sinks to 10 cents-a-pound, the price of pork doesn't budge a dime. A farmer told me he watched a woman buy a ham for $18 this winter and thought to himself, "Another $10 would buy the whole hog if she got a live one."

Some of that's the price we pay for having our food cut, wrapped, and delivered in its most convenient form; and some of it isn't. Most folks wouldn't know what to do with a whole pig, though, especially if they had to haul it home in their car.

I've been down that road and so has my friend Virgil. Some years ago Virgil's daughter owned a pig for her 4-H project. One day he realized the pig wasn't growing fast enough and needed to go to the auction instead of the live-stock show.

Virgil did what most of us would have done — under-estimated a pig. He left work early and headed out to the farm where his daughter kept the pig.

Nobody had a truck available on short notice, so Virgil decided his Chevy Blazer would have to do. Loading the pig was easy. Virgil just opened the back door, grabbed the pig in a bear hug, and hoisted him in.

He put some straw in the back, but the pig exuded a lot more odor than one might imagine. So Virgil rolled the front windows down to get some fresh air.

Everything went fine for awhile. Then, the pig decided he needed some air, too, and proceeded to crawl over the back seat.

Pretty soon the pig noticed no one was sitting on the passenger side in the front. You know how that is, there's no point riding in coach when you can upgrade to first class. So the pig moved up.

Virgil was too busy driving to do anything about the pig, and the smell was getting pretty thick. He figured the sooner he got the pig to the auction yard the better.

Just as they reached the edge of town, the pig decided maybe he could help with the driving. That's when Virgil realized things were getting out of hand.

He got the pig in a headlock with his free arm and tried to reason with it. When he stopped at the first stop sign, a car pulled up beside him. Virgil looked straight ahead — hoping he wouldn't see anyone he knew.

By the time he got to the second stop sign his whole attitude had changed. Now he was looking for anyone he might know. He needed some help with this @#*$* pig!

Finally Virgil got the pig to the auction yard. He thought that was the end of the story. But it wasn't.

Some of Virgil's friends got such a kick out of this unfortunate episode, they hired an artist to paint the whole scene on the cafe window downtown. Then everyone in town got to see how he looked driving down the street with his arm around a pig.

What does all of this have to do with economics? I don't know, but it might help illustrate why it's still cheaper for most folks to get their pork chops at the grocery.

Uncle Harry

This era of medical miracles has created some confusion about aging, but there's no question exercise is good for a person. I look at some of the farmers and others who work outdoors and think, "There's no way that man can be as old as he says he is."

On the other hand, some folks just age better than others. The fellow we called "Uncle Harry" is a good example.

Harry was retired before I met him, and I have no idea what he did for a living. I know what he did for retirement, though: He went fishing.

And when he wasn't fishing, he was hunting. My first recollection of Uncle Harry was the time he and my brother Kenny came to my house for a quail hunt.

Uncle Harry was somewhere in his late seventies then, but one would never guess his age by watching him in the field. We started out at 9:00 AM and he was still going strong late in the day.

I owned two bird dogs at the time but generally hunted them one at a time. We hunted with the Brittany spaniel that morning and were close to limits by noon.

Uncle Harry was pleased. "I think I'll buy that dog a bag of food. If it weren't for him, we'd be going hungry right now," he declared.

This made my day, of course. Anyone who owns bird dogs can tell you a lot of things are said about these creatures, and the majority of it isn't very nice. One tends to savor the good times.

We went to the house for lunch, and I put the Brittany in his pen. After lunch, I released my English setter, Goldie.

This dog was wired! She left the pen like a bullet and circled the house three times before touching down. If tornadoes were white and orange Goldie would have been a storm.

I read a lot of sports magazines in those days and knew having a fresh dog is vital for quail hunting. The rich guys keep four dogs in their wagon and only hunt each one for an hour or so.

Uncle Harry looked at my brother and said. "What is that boy doing?! We just got one dog tired enough we could hunt with him, and now he gets out a new one!"

A couple of years later Kenny and Uncle Harry were pheasant hunting near our home town when they noticed a guy hoofing it across the field toward them. The two hunters had just crossed a creek bottom and didn't see this fellow until he was about a hundred yards away.

It was the game warden. He had been following them for quite awhile and was huffing and puffing something fierce when he finally caught up.

The warden asked to see their hunting licenses. He looked at Uncle Harry's license and noticed his birth date was 1886. (This was nearly 30 years ago.)

"My God man, you're over 80 years old!? It was all I could do to catch up with you!" the game warden said.

Uncle Harry looked at the warden and said, "If we had seen you coming, you wouldn't have gotten anywhere near this close."

Ra-a-alph

It was a beautiful flight in a little four-seater, but I could see that problems were brewing. My wife had never been in such a small plane, and her tendency toward motion sickness is well-documented.

"Better take your Dramamine," I said. "Do you want to ride in the front?"

"No, I think I'll be O.K. in the back," Connie said.

"Sure, you'll be fine," the captain said.

"Dramamine makes you drowsy," the captain's wife added.

"There are worse things than being drowsy," I thought. "Lots worse. Like Ralph, the God of motion sickness, for one thing."

I've spent several fishing trips hanging over the rail because I didn't take my dramamine. Now, I don't get on the boat or in a small plane without it (unless I forget of course).

We were airborne about an hour when I noticed Connie wasn't doing very well. "How ya feelin'?" I asked. "Did you see that waterfall down there?"

"Ra-a-al-ph!" she said.

"Want some Dramamine?" I asked.

"Ra-a-al-ph. Ra-a-alph," she replied.

My mind jogged back to those deep-sea fishing trips when I was barely out of the harbor before I began chumming. I remembered the advice friends had given me. "Look at the horizon." "Don't look down." "Eat a good breakfast." "Don't eat breakfast." "Go to bed early." "Stay up all night." "Eat something salty." "Don't eat." "Dramamine makes you drowsy."

One particular trip stands out in memory. I was with a group of co-workers, and we had the entire charter boat to ourselves.

The first thing we did was set up a pool with prizes for the first fish, biggest fish, and the first sick. I lost out on all three.

We had barely started fishing when I lost my breakfast. "I win! I win!" I shouted. "I'm 'first sick'!"

"Too late," Bill said. "Craig got sick 10 minutes ago."

Then I noticed everyone on the boat had the same name. "Pass the crackers — Ra-a-alph." "Did you see that pelican? Ra-a-alph, Ra-a-alph." "Fish on! Ra-a-a-alph, Ra-a-alph, Ra-a-alph!"

Soon I was getting advice from everyone who wasn't sick yet. Friends, enemies, and fellow fish feeders advised, "Look at the horizon." "Don't look down." "Don't look up." "Eat some crackers." "Think pleasant thoughts."

I tried them all, but I ran out of pleasant thoughts quicker than anything. Looking back I wish someone had said, "Take your Dramamine."

That's the only thing that works for me. I'll bet it would work for Connie, too; if she ever gets in one of those little planes again.

Tangled In The Web

It seems everyone wants to drag us into the information age. I've made up my mind: I'm not going!

First we got faster computers, then call waiting and fax machines. Now it's voice mail, e-mail, and the World Wide Web.

I can't complain about computers. I love computers, but some of this other stuff has been oversold it seems to me.

Consider how folks would react if this technology were reversed. What if the internet was fifty years old, and the telephone was brand new?

Wouldn't it be great to call people up, listen to their voices, talk as fast as you want, and get an answer immediately? What a great invention — the telephone.

Then, imagine having to type a note or letter, leave it on someone's machine, and wait for them to type a note or letter in response. That's what we do with e-mail: Send folks a note and then call them up to make sure they got it.

It's better than a telegram. At least we don't have to learn Morse Code.

How about fax machines? The fax machine always reminds me of public relations agencies I used to write for.

The PR agencies wanted everything by overnight mail. No matter what it was, it had to go overnight.

So, we mailed their stuff overnight and charged them another $12. Then, when I hadn't heard anything for a couple of weeks, I would call them up.

Nine times out of ten, the person who received the overnight copy hadn't read it. He was on vacation, had his appendix removed, or his dog ate the mail.

That's where the fax machine comes in. The fax lets us transmit copy instantly — because we were too disorganized to mail it a couple of days sooner.

This week I read that companies in Italy and Japan are making refrigerators and ovens featuring internet access. The Japanese "internet refrigerator" has more computing power than most PC's and keeps your vegetables cold at the same time. I don't know what a refrigerator computes, but it should be able to tell us when the cheese turns green.

This smart fridge is controlled by a touch panel on the door, or verbally through a built-in microphone. Experts say American consumers will prefer the touch panel over the microphone. Most of us are used to talking to an open fridge, but giving commands through the door is just another way to frighten the kids.

The "intelligent oven" is supposed to take over where the internet refrigerator leaves off. This oven will pull a recipe from the internet and cook a roast for us. (Provided we remembered to buy the roast.)

How can we remember to buy the roast? I can't speak for others, but I just put a note on my refrigerator.

How To Bawrie An Arn

A recent telephone conversation reminded me of the many dialects spoken in different parts of the country. My caller was from Maryland but had that silky, smooth accent I associate with parts further south.

I really enjoy listening to the Southern dialect, but I'm not very good at picking-up inflections. I found myself asking this woman to spell nearly every word of the addresses she was providing me.

I must have seemed senile asking her to spell words like "Court," "Trail," and "Borough."

Just to show how inept I am on the telephone, I once asked my niece to spell her name so I could give her message to my wife! It was a little voice, after all, and Connie teaches school. I thought it was one of her students.

Still, I'm not as tone-deaf as the New York City hotel clerks I heard about recently. These fellows have definitely been in the city too long.

My wife heard the story while dining in a North Carolina restaurant. Several women at a nearby table were recounting their recent trips and excursions.

These ladies were laughing and having a wonderful time, but I couldn't really hear what they were saying. When we left the restaurant, Connie asked, "Did you hear that woman's story about the arn?"

"No," I told her. "I heard parts of stories, but I never could get the whole thing."

My wife said this lady and some of her friends had taken a trip to New York City last year. It was their first trip to the Big Apple, but they got to the hotel in fine fashion and finished unpacking in no time.

Then, the entire group trooped down to the lobby. They sent one lady over to talk to the desk clerk.

"Ah'd lack to bawrie and arn," she said.

The clerk took a step backward. "Pardon me, Madam," he said.

"An arn," she repeated. "Ah'd lack to bawrie and arn."

"Hey, Charlie," the clerk yelled to a second man behind the desk. "Come over here and listen to this."

Charlie walked over, and the southern lady said, "An arn. Ah'd lack to bawrie an arn!" her voice beginning to tremble.

The two clerks called the manager out of his office. The lady from North Carolina repeated her request.

"Could you spell that, please," the manager asked.

"A-h-h, Ahr, O, Ee-en," the woman said.

The three men just stared at each other. The manager grabbed a piece of paper and said, "Here, write it out."

The woman wrote, "IRON! I'D LIKE TO BORROW AN IRON!"

"Oh! Of course," the manager blustered. "An arn! We'll bring that up to your room immediately."

Choose Your Rut Carefully

Spring is a busy time for high school seniors. They're planning for graduation, looking for summer jobs (or full time jobs), and wondering how many classes they can skip before somebody catches them.

Most of all these kids are getting lots of advice. "Be sure to get home before it's too late; and don't drive around without any gas in the car." That kind of stuff.

It's no wonder kids become stressed, even irrational, at this time of year. All that advice begins to to wear on a person after awhile.

That's what happened when my son was in high school many years ago. Russ was about to graduate and had talked to an army recruiter once or twice during the spring.

His mother and I supported the idea, but joining the armed services is an important decision. Not something to rush into.

So I started giving advice. "You'll have to make your own decision," I counseled. "But you might want to talk to the Navy and Air Force recruiters before you rush into anything."

"No, I've made up my mind," Russ said. "I'm going to join the army. I'm tired of people telling me what to do."

That's why advice should be given in small doses, like the letter my Uncle Willis wrote for graduating seniors in 1956. I received the letter this week from a man who attended school at Ansonia, Ohio, where my uncle was superintendent for many years.

This fellow has been reading my stuff in an Indiana paper and gradually decided the Pond writing the column might be related to his high school superintendent, Willis Pond. He was right, of course, and his correspondence was greatly appreciated.

I believe my uncle's letter was printed in the Ansonia High School Yearbook. I'm going to share it with you because I think it's as good today as it was then.

"Dear Seniors:

"Long ago and far away in the midwestern country there once stood a road sign at a spot where a side road left the main road. One who has lived in our American middlewest of forty years ago can readily understand; but it will be hard for one who has known only our modern improved highways to visualize such a situation.

"Nevertheless the condition was standard and the sign was real, and it read as follows: 'Choose your rut carefully; you will be in it for the next twenty miles.'

"As I write these lines for the 1956 Ansonia Oracle, I am tempted to repeat this wise advice with, of course, a slight variation. I would address it to the Seniors of 1956 and it would read thusly: 'Choose your rut carefully; you may be in it for the rest of your life.' I will not insult your intelligence by enlarging upon the subject; you know what I mean."

Very truly yours,
Willis V. Pond
Superintendent

Recycle Your Jugs

"Do you have any boxes that say 'recycled paper' on them? I need something for school that says 'recycled paper'," my wife said.

"You won't find anything like that in my office," I told her. "This ain't no recycling place. This is a gol durn writin' place."

I glanced at the boxes and packages strewn around my office floor and noticed none of them said "Recycled," "100% Natural," or "Made From Trees That Were Already Dead."

My boxes say things like "Keep Out of Reach of Children," "90 Proof, Guaranteed," "Do Not Open Near Flame," "Run For Your Life, If You Know What's Good For You!"

My unkempt office and surly attitude remind me of a fellow who used to run a tavern near the little town where I grew up. This man knew how to be cranky, too, and mornings were his worst time of day.

One Sunday morning the tavern owner was leaning on the end of his bar, when the front door flew open and a pert, little lady popped-in from a nearby campground.

"I need four deli sandwiches: One ham with Swiss cheese

on rye, two ham with American on sourdough, and one roast beef with Swiss on white bread," she said.

The tavern owner wasn't feeling good. He hadn't shaved, his hair wasn't combed, and his shirt was unbuttoned to his waist. He wasn't expecting any strangers.

The tavern man bit his lip and peered across the bar at the happy camper. "Look, lady," he said. "This ain't no #@$* eatin' place. This is a #$@ $#@& drinkin' place!"

The only customer present that day says the spritely lady turned on her heels and went through the front door so fast the hinges were still rattling as she drove away.

What does this have to do with recycling? Nothing, but I thought it was a pretty good story, anyway.

Speaking of recycling, I know I should be more environmentally friendly (or even more friendly would help); but I just can't get worked-up about reclaiming everything.

A few weeks ago I talked with a man who works at a landfill in another state. He says his company is required by law to recycle anything someone wants to see recycled.

A year or so ago somebody decided the company should recycle plastic milk jugs. So this fellow and his crew constructed a building to store plastic jugs until they could be compacted.

After the building was full of milk containers, the company brought in a compactor — and two men spent half-a-day mashing jugs. When they finished they had a block of plastic weighing about 800 pounds.

Compacted milk jugs are worth $2 per ton if I remember the story correctly. This means the landfill company built the shed, rented a compactor, and paid several men's wages to reclaim 80 cents worth of milk jugs.

What does this have to do with the tavern owner? Nothing, but it just goes to show you some stories are too short for an entire column.

Beware The Passengers

Everyone is harping about the airlines these days. Flights are late, luggage is lost, and somebody told Aunt Emma to go sit down before she has another hemorrhage. What is air travel coming to?

Why can't the planes fly on time? And how do the baggage handlers always mash my bag of peaches? I wrapped it with duct tape!

Two of the major complaints from airline consumers are late flights and canceled flights. The U.S Bureau of Transportation reports one-third of all flights arriving at the airport nearest my home were late for the month of June. (Anything over 15 minutes is considered late.)

United Airlines had the worst record in June. Maybe their pilots' strike had something to do with that?

It would be nice to see more data. A spokesman for the Bureau of Transportation explains the report for July flights should have been ready the first week of August, but a change in mainframe computers delayed the report for three weeks.

I'm happy the Bureau of Transportation isn't running an

airline. Three weeks is a long time to wait for a flight.

I can't speak for others; but I've flown on quite a few airplanes, and I think the service is pretty good. I don't especially like the food, but a lot of people do. Besides, I'm not on there to eat.

I appreciate the airlines' emphasis on safety, too. When I board a plane, I always tell the pilot, "Don't worry about being a little late. Take plenty of time for gas. Let me know if you need any help checking the tires."

The scariest thing about air travel is the passengers, as far as I'm concerned. You never know what they're going to do.

There's always some guy with an 80-pound carry-on who wants to stuff it into the overhead bin. He needs a huge carry-on bag so he won't have to wait on luggage like the rest of us.

And I'll never forget the woman with a big wicker basket strapped on her back. She had been shopping and all of her stuff was in the basket. I've always wondered if that basket was the first purchase of her vacation or the last.

The flight attendant was extremely polite as she explained where the basket needed to go. Many of the passengers would have been more graphic.

This woman inspired images of a grueling portage by a French fur trapper. I was just happy to see she didn't bring the canoe.

Then we have those passengers who are rude to folks who are doing their best to help them. Readers may recall the man who got testy with the clerk checking his baggage.

The clerk smiled and said nothing as the passenger griped about the lousy service the airline was providing. When he left, the next customer asked, "How could you put up with such a pompous idiot?"

"Oh, it's pretty easy," the clerk said. "That man is flying to Dallas, but his luggage is headed for Syracuse."

The Doctor Knows Best

This has been a bad year for colds. I got a nasty cold before Christmas, finally got rid of it in January, and caught it again in February.

I don't know if a person can catch the same cold twice, but it sure feels the same. I probably should go to the doctor, but you know how that is.

I grew up in the days of the old country doctors, and you didn't go see them if you didn't have to. Our doctors were always nice people, but their treatments were a little scary sometimes.

We have to give the old doctors credit, though. They knew when to treat you and when to leave you alone.

That's how it was when a bunch of fellows from town got together for a fishing trip on Lake Erie. Our town wasn't very big. So it didn't matter if you were the doctor, minister, or a suspected horse thief; everyone was invited for the big fishing trip.

Most of the men in town went, including my dad and brother. They provided this eyewitness account.

Spirits were high as the charter left the dock and headed for open water. Everyone chipped-in with a dollar for first fish, most fish, and biggest fish.

Doc suggested they have a pool for first sick, too; seeing as how he would probably get that money one way or another. This drew a big laugh from everyone. Everyone except Ralph, the town banker.

Ralph came along for the camaraderie. He was feeling the sway of the boat more than most.

The captain cut the engine, and the boat began to drift with the waves. Ralph reached in his pocket for some Dramamine.

Soon they were into fish. Nothing big, but a few walleye and some perch. My brother, Kenny, caught a walleye and unhooked another for Dad.

The second fish was hooked pretty deep, and Kenny got some blood on his arm. The blood didn't bother him, but it had a noticeable effect on Ralph.

He had given up fishing and was sitting in a deck chair, staring at the horizon. Ralph looked kind of puny, and his coloring was bad. His normally ruddy complexion had turned to ashen gray.

Soon it was lunch time. My brother got out the boxed chicken furnished by the charter. He took out a drumstick and began to gnaw on it.

Dad looked over at Ralph. The combination of fish blood on Kenny's arm and the chicken leg in his hand was the last straw for the banker. His gray turned to green.

Dad yelled at Doc. "Hey, Doc. Do you suppose there's anything you can do for Ralph here?"

Doc put down his fishing rod and made a big scene of examining the patient. Then he said solemnly, "I'm afraid there's nothing I can do."

"What he's going to do, he can do all by himself."

Impersonating A Cowboy

Good news, Western clothes are back in style. Bad news, the price of boots just got another shot of steroids.

Retailers say having a President from Texas and Vice-president from Wyoming has hoisted sales of Western wear. News reports say President Bush wore boots to the inauguration, and many of the women attending that event were wearing boots under those long, velvet dresses.

Retailers say folks who care about fashion are now trying for the cowboy look. That kind of defeats the whole image as far as I'm concerned.

Cowboys don't care about fashion. That's why they've been wearing the same clothes all of these years.

Anybody who cares about fashion will never look like a cowboy. President Bush doesn't look like a cowboy, nor does Cheney. They just like Western clothes.

Al Gore wears boots, too, but he doesn't look like any sort of rancher — or even a country boy. Al needs the boots to keep his socks clean.

I wouldn't mind looking like a cowboy, but I can't do it.

Neither can those other guys.

Cowboy impersonators will learn there's more to the image than buying clothes. You've got to have a truck, for one thing — and some cows. Not very many, but you've got to have some.

A person actually needs two trucks to appear legitimate, a big truck for the cows and a small one for the dogs. The smaller truck is called a "rig."

Don't forget the dogs.   A cowboy needs a real dog, not one of those squeaky, little mutts that sounds like he needs a shot of oil, or a big German shepherd that eats more than a cow does.

A cowboy needs a cowdog — like an Australian shepherd or a Dingo. Dogs that can stand in the gate and scare cows all over creation.

Then, once you get the cows and the dogs, you put the dogs and two bales of hay in the rig and head into town. (The hay goes in the back. Dogs can go front or back, unless your state requires seat belts for dogs.)

Why two bales of hay? That's pretty obvious when you think about it. Three bales looks like you're showing off, and one bale looks like you forgot the other one.

Where does a person get the hay? Some folks grow their own, but it's easier to just buy some of those sticks the neighbor bales up. That way you don't have to own all that machinery.

Where can you get a cowdog? That's easy, too, you just head down to the pound and take your pick. Any dog with beady, little eyes and pointy ears was probably a cowdog at one time or another.

Why does animal control have so many cowdogs? Mainly because these dogs all answer to the same name.

The dog catcher just drives around yelling, "Git in the pickup you stupid #@* *#@$ *&$#@&," and he's got all of the cowdogs in the country, slick as a whistle.

A Bitter Pill

I'm having a difficult time with the many vitamin, mineral, and herbal supplements on the market these days. How is a person supposed to know which pills to take and how much is enough?

During the past few weeks I've been reading about St. Johnswort, ginko, and ginseng, to name a few. I understand these are all good, but I'm always afraid of product interactions.

St. Johnswort is said to be a "mood enhancer" that helps fight depression. Ginko reportedly increases blood flow to the brain, improving memory and math skills. Ginseng is supposed to boost energy and possibly memory as well.

What if I take all three? I might jump out of bed in a wonderful mood, remember my deadlines, add up my bills, and go back into another depression. Maybe I should stick with the mood enhancers.

I was surprised when I first heard about St. Johnswort. I remember St. Johnswort (Hypericum perforatum) as a weedy plant that causes blistering around the mouth and eyes of livestock unlucky enough to eat it — and then stand around in direct sunlight.

I'm told St. Johnswort pills are made from a different

plant in the same family. The label cautions, however, "Because of its photosensitizing properties, avoid long exposure to direct sunlight, tanning lights, or ultra-violet light sources while taking this product."

Direct sunlight?! That's where I go fishing. If you want to see a guy in a bad mood, just tell me I can't go fishing.

We used to consult doctors about medications and nutritional supplements, but now folks are realizing doctors are not trained nutritionists. Many don't trust their doctor for nutritional advice.

We do trust neighbors, cousins, health food salesmen, and radio commentators for this advice, however. I find that confusing.

So I did what any confused, married person would do. I asked my wife, "O.K., if I take St. Johnswort, will I be a better person? The bottle says 'Mood Enhancer'."

"It certainly couldn't hurt you any," she said.

"The label says to take one caplet, one to three times daily. Does that mean I should take one, two, or three?"

"The maximum should be about right for you," she quipped.

This reminds me of a James Thurber story in which a woman wrote Thurber to ask about the best food for writers. She had been told fish is "brain food," and wondered if eating fish would improve her writing. She also inquired about the best type of fish for writers.

Thurber wrote back, saying fish was indeed "brain food" and excellent fare for aspiring writers. As for the type of fish, he suggested a whale should be about right in this instance.

Now, where was I? Oh yes, reading a St. Johnswort bottle. This is a natural product, so I was naturally curious about its contents.

The label says this product contains Dicalcium Phosphate, Microcrystaline Cellulose, Calcium Carbonate, Crosarmellose Sodium, Crospovidone, Hydrogenated Cottonseed Oil, Sodium Hydroxide, Hydroxypropyl, Cellulose, Polyethylene Glycol, Docusate Sodium, Titanium Dioxide, Red 40 Lake, Blue 2 Lake, and Carnauba Wax.

What's all that stuff?! Who knows? I'm just happy it's natural.

Gopher Broke

It happens every fall, like the song of the crickets and the geese flying north: My wife looks at her flower beds and exclaims, "The gophers are back! Why don't you do something about them?"

"I am doing something," I tell her. "I'm ignoring them."

I've tried everything else. Traps, water, guns, voodoo. I even held a contest asking readers to submit their best ideas for controlling gophers.

Folks suggested pouring water down their burrows, siccing the dog on them, creating vibrations with whirley gigs. One person described a sport called "gopher spinning."

My wife chewed-up some gum and put that in the burrows, on the theory that gophers like to chew gum and will eat it until their bowels clog-up.

"Why chew the gum before stuffing it in the burrows?" I asked. "Let the gophers chew their own gum."

Then, I received a newspaper clipping from a reader in Alaska. The clipping describes a Colorado man who specializes in prairie dog control.

This fellow bought an old truck that had been used for pumping sewage lines around Denver. Then, he converted it into a prairie dog extractor.

Now, he drives up to a prairie dog town, inserts the truck's hose into a burrow, and fills his tank with rodents. This man sells prairie dogs to pet stores in Japan.

What does this have to do with gophers? I'm not sure, but anyone with a huge vacuum cleaner and a market for miniature prairie dogs should call me right away.

After years of frustration I think I've solved my wife's gopher problem. I have concluded her gophers are probably moles.

I should have known, but these moles don't act like the moles I used to know. These critters raise the ground up in spots, but much of their burrow is deeper underground.

The experts claim you can eliminate insects in your lawn and the moles will go away, but I'm not so sure. Ours go away every fall and come back the next year.

A man I saw on television has a more violent solution. When the TV crews approached, this fellow was sitting in his pasture, watching an active mole hill.

His elbows are braced against his knees, and a nickel-plated .38 rests securely between his hands. "When you see the dirt move, you have to shoot straight down the hole. Otherwise, you'll miss 'em," he said.

Cameras zoomed closer while he stared intently at the mole hill. Suddenly, Ka-boom! "Rats, missed another one," he said.

I thought about that, but I bought a mole trap instead. There's something about sitting in your flower bed with a .38 revolver that makes the neighbors nervous.

Advice For Investors

A person can learn a lot by reading the newspaper. One has to be careful not to believe everything he reads, but there's no question the paper is full of information.

The investment section has become my favorite part of the big dailies in recent years. I used to read the comics first, but have decided reading the financial advice puts me in a better mood to understand the funnies.

The thing I enjoy most about investment columnists is the confidence they exude. I have yet to see a financial writer with any amount of humility.

If a person writes the investment advisor and asks what they should do with their life savings, the columnist tells them flat out: "Put your money into mutual funds. These should provide enough income to have a good time — and the security you'll need if you break a leg in the process."

A person who is near retirement is supposed to choose conservative funds. A younger person should select more aggressive funds.

This advice is based on the universally accepted principle that folks should invest according to how much money they want, and how soon they want it.

Financial advisors say people who are nearing retirement should be conservative, because they will need some of their investment money fairly soon. These folks don't have time to ride out the highs and lows of the stock market.

A younger person, on the other hand, has many years before they need this money. They can flirt with more aggressive investments, on the assumption that everything goes up in the long run, and even a blind hog finds an acorn sooner or later.

This is good advice, I think. The stock market has been going up (on the average) for more than 50 years, and anyone who remembers more history than that should stay away from it.

Most intriguing for me is the widespread belief that investments should reflect a person's personality, as well as how much money he or she needs.

Every few weeks the investment columnist receives a letter from someone who wants to retire in 10 years and needs another half-million dollars to do it with.

The advisor will say, "In order to meet your goal of early retirement, you'll need some aggressive investments that return about 18% per year. That's O.K., though, if you are comfortable with a fair amount of risk."

I would be more direct and tell them, "That's great if you think you can pick the right nags for all the races. Otherwise, you might have to work a bit longer."

Washington D.C.?!

The idea of ranking cities for livability has taken an ugly turn. A study released last week concludes Washington D.C. is the best city in the U.S. in which to live.

Authors of the study say crime rates, educational opportunities, and clean water are a few of the many criteria considered in their livability rankings. I can't quibble with the educational opportunities around Washington D.C., but the water in that town must be a crime of some sort.

My impression of the latest city ranking is that the authors were reading their list upside down. Maybe my criteria are different from theirs.

If I were ranking cities, small towns would come out on top, and most cities wouldn't even make the list. My criteria for a nice city leans heavily on social amenities: Does the coffee shop give free refills? Are the mechanics friendly?

My livability index would compute the population of a community and divide by 10. If this number is over 1,000, we subtract 10 points for overcrowding.

I would count the households in town and estimate the

'secats. If the number of cats exceeds the num-
ve deduct 5 points.

..y ranking system looks at transportation. Can
ₒct where you want to go and find a parking space when
you get there?

Does your community have parking garages with capacity for more than two cars? If "no," add 10 points.

Does the community have mass transit, or does everyone have to ride their own horse? Does everyone have a horse? If "yes," add five points.

How far do you have to drive to find some decent hay? Can you find a horseshoer when you need one?

Consider the recreational opportunities. Is there good fishing within 20 miles of town?

If the answer is "yes," add 10 points. If the answer is "no," move.

Do folks own guns for hunting, or for protection? Can most residents distinguish a cow from a moose?

What about cultural opportunities? How far does a person have to drive to attend the symphony or the opera? If these events are more than 50 miles away, add 5 points.

If the miles to good fishing are less than miles to the opera, add 5 more points and go fishing.

What about education? Can folks go to school if they want to? Do kids go to school, even when they don't want to? If the answer is "yes," add 10 points.

Are students excused from school for county fairs and livestock shows? If "no," subtract 10 points.

I applied this test to my community and got a score of 35. I won't say where we lost points, but we outscored Washington D.C. by 55.

A Vast Conspiracy

I don't think I'll ever understand politics. I was just beginning to accept that vast right wing conspiracy theory, when suddenly we've switched gears. Now we've got people talking about left wing conspiracies.

I always have to stop and ask, "O.K., the left wing is the liberals, and the right wing is conservative, but which ones are the communists?"

The whole thing reminds me of a cattle rancher I used to see quite often. This fellow (we'll call him Albert) knew the left wingers from the right wingers better than anyone I've ever known.

If Albert were here today he would say, "Those liberals we send to Washington D.C. wouldn't know a vast conspiracy if they saw one. This isn't half of that. This is more like a half-vast conspiracy."

I bumped into Albert many years ago when I stopped at the grocery to buy a newspaper. Our little town had a local paper, and we had two major dailies delivered from out of town. One of the daily papers was large and liberal, while the other was small and more conservative.

Albert noticed I was buying the liberal paper and nearly fainted. "How far left can you get?" he asked.

"Oh?! I don't plan to read it. I just use it for starting fires," I told him.

I should confess I always buy the bigger newspaper. That's one of the paradoxes of my conservatism: I don't like the liberal paper, but I buy it because it weighs more. It seems like a better value.

Albert was more strict in his conservatism. He wasn't very fond of environmentalists, and someone who writes a newspaper column, as I do, might be termed a "syndicated communist."

He was a good-natured fellow, though, and nobody was ever offended. I should say nobody except the sheriff's deputies. They might have been offended once or twice.

Albert had a tenuous relationship with the sheriff's office. His cattle roamed over large tracts of timberland, and they were constantly getting lost, shot, and/or butchered.

Then, he would call the sheriff's office, and they would send someone out to investigate. The sheriff's deputies did their best, but solving these cow mysteries was no easy task.

A deputy's inability to find the culprit would cause Albert to remark, "Those sheriff's deputies couldn't track an elephant with a nosebleed in two feet of snow."

One night I was sitting with a group of ranchers around a meeting table, when Albert said, "Somebody butchered another one of my calves the other day."

"Did you report it to the sheriff?" one of the ranchers asked.

"Yeah, I called them up," Albert said. "But they've got a smart aleck young deputy in there; and when I told him who it was he hung up on me!"

Just Go Fishing

The sport of fishing gets more complicated each year. Times have changed since the day I walked into the hardware store to buy my first fly rod.

I was earning 50 cents a week in those days, and Dad agreed to pay me several weeks in advance to put me in the market for a fishing outfit. I hiked down to the hardware store after school and selected an eight-foot fly rod with an automatic reel made by South Bend. Then, I bought some E-level line and a bunch of flies with beads on their heads.

There's no question that was the most miserable set of fishing equipment a kid has ever assembled. The line was much too light for the rod and those automatic reels were just like a runaway window blind.

I kept the reel wound as tight as I could get it — and each time I hit the retrieve lever that reel would guzzle line like an anteater eating spaghetti.

My rod cost $10, and the reel was about the same, bringing the total outfit to around $20. Looking back I can see the rod and reel cost me almost a year's salary — about the same as fishing costs me today.

I caught fish on that rod, though; and the reel would bring them in, too. One squeeze on that retrieve button, and I had a fish with a rod tip half way to his belly button.

Those were the days before everyone had a bunch of fancy equipment. We just grabbed a pole and a few worms and rode our bikes down to the fishing hole.

Nowadays folks spend two days gathering up equipment and drive 300 miles looking for a place to fish — and a dock big enough to unload a 20-foot boat. Then we zip around the lake wondering where the fish are.

I can't speak for others, but I've learned a curious thing about fishing. I've noticed the more equipment I get the fewer fish I catch.

I thought this was a coincidence at first; the fishing probably isn't what it used to be. Maybe I'm fishing in the wrong places.

The fact remains, though; the more I get, the less I catch.

Finally, I think I've solved the puzzle. A person who just jumps on his bike and heads for the fishing hole spends a lot of time fishing, whereas a guy who works 50 hours a week to pay for his equipment spends a lot of time in his cubicle.

Therefore, I've adopted the philosophy of an old Swedish taxidermist my brother met years ago. My brother landed a very nice bass at a lake in Minnesota and took it to the taxidermist for mounting.

As he was leaving, Kenny asked the taxidermist, "How long will it take to get the fish mounted?"

"It all depends," the old Swede said. "It should be about three months — if I don't get too busy.

"If I get too busy, it could be forever. 'Cause ven I get too busy, I don't do nothin'. I yust go fishing."

Pets And Their People

I am a firm believer in the old theory that people tend to resemble their pets. Or, to put it another way, pets sometimes look like their people.

This is especially true for dogs, I think. Nobody resembles a cat. There's something about the big, round head and flattened face of a cat that humans have trouble imitating.

Dogs are easy, though, as I learned in chemistry class many years ago. This was one of those huge college lectures where students sit in an elevated semicircle with stairs leading down to the stage where the professor holds sway.

Class was about to convene when the girl next to me said, "Have you heard about the theory that people look like their pets. It's true, and I'll bet you anything our professor has a German shepherd."

"That's absurd," I thought. "Who ever heard of people looking like their dogs?"

I kept my mouth shut, though, and glanced down at the stage where our instructor was adjusting her microphone. Sure enough, the chemistry professor's short black hair, with a tinge of gray around her muzzle, gave a definite likeness to a German shepherd!

A veterinarian might have guessed the professor to be around five years old. No longer a pup, but still strong in the jaw and alert of eye. I would think twice before turning my back on her.

Then, I glanced at the co-ed who made this outrageous connection. With her round face and long, fluffy hair this girl was a dead ringer for a cocker spaniel!

I could imagine her romping through the fields, chasing meadowlarks, sniffing the wind, and rolling in the cockleburs. I worried about her temperament and wondered if she might snap at a person who said the wrong thing.

Then I remembered my old beagle, Smokey, with his short, stubby legs and wry, little grin. I always felt sorry for Smokey. Some days even the rabbits laughed at him.

Soon I had forgotten all about chemistry, and was wondering if people might have similarities to other livestock, as well as their dogs.

Are horse owners strong and athletic? Beef producers tough and determined?

What about folks who raise rabbits? (I don't even want to know.)

I'm sure this theory could be carried too far. There must be some very nice folks raising alligators. And hog producers I've known are generally rather skinny.

Sheep ranchers are the most independent people in the world, and fish farmers may be afraid of the water. Even the dog and people theory is far from foolproof.

A few folks might be offended at being compared to an animal, such as their dog. But let's face it, the dogs may not be thrilled about it, either.

Don't Forget The Manure

This is an exciting time for gardeners. Everyone has been cooped up all winter, seed catalogs are arriving in the mail, and nurseries are stocking their shelves. It just seems natural to get outside and plant something.

We must not be fooled, however. Experienced gardeners know it's too early for many gardening activities, too late for others, and maybe we should just lie down here and think about this for a month or two.

Everything I read about gardening reminds me how much this activity has changed over the years. Folks used to buy a few seeds, plant them in a hotbed, and then nurse those seedlings for weeks.

Now, the majority of gardeners head straight for the nursery. Then, they grab a little, red wagon, fill it with bags of potting soil and some half-grown plants, and drop $60 at the cash register on the way out.

That's not gardening, that's shopping! Whatever happened to the days when gardens helped a family save money?

Whatever happened to the days when hotbeds were filled

with loam and horse manure, rather than $40 worth of potting soil. I'm afraid our modern gardeners have forgotten all about economics — and horse manure as well.

The best example of this lapse of memory is a woman from California who moved to the country and decided to buy a horse. She knew nothing about horses, but figured riding would be fun, and the manure would be great for her garden.

Her only problem was a lack of space; so she started looking for a farm that boards horses. This woman understood farmers and ranchers can be suspicious of newcomers, so she kept her mouth shut as much as possible.

The first stable she visited said they charged $80 per month to board a horse. "Veterinary fees are extra, and we keep the manure," the horse wrangler told her.

"Oh, but I want the manure for my garden," she said.

"I'm sorry, Ma'am, that's not the way we do business," the horseman replied.

When she arrived at the second stable the owner said, "We charge $75 a month, vet fees are extra, our farrier changes shoes every four months, and we get the manure."

"Oh, I hope the farrier changes the horse's shoes, too," she quipped, but no one laughed.

By the time she arrived at a third stable, the California woman was better prepared. She knew horses are expensive to feed, she could expect some vet bills, and the manure is apparently quite valuable.

The third stable owner told her, "Our boarding fee is $30 a month, you pay the vet bills, and shoeing costs are extra."

The woman was so pleased with the low price, she almost forgot about the manure. Suddenly she remembered, "Oh, who gets the manure?" she asked.

The stable owner pushed his hat to one side and said, "Ma'am, for $30 a month there ain't gonna be any manure!"

Strangers In The Cafe

Racial profiling has been much in the news recently. City police departments are spending a lot of time determining if racial bias is a factor in deciding who gets stopped for traffic violations — and how folks are treated after they're stopped.

I think most departments might as well admit they have a problem and get busy trying to fix it. It's probably not possible to eliminate all biases, however.

We're all guilty of profiling in various forms. I find myself engaging in gender profiling, age profiling, and eighteen-year-old kid driving a red Corvette with the top down profiling.

Folks who live in farm communities are probably as subject to profiling as anyone. I've walked down the streets of San Francisco with the strong conviction that everyone around me thought I had just fallen off the last turnip truck.

And I've sat in farm country cafes with the certain knowledge I was the only stranger (foreigner) in the place. One can almost hear people on the street, "There's a stranger in the cafe. There's a stranger in the cafe!"

I look at the floor and wonder if my boots are too shiny. Then,

I thank my lucky stars I'm not wearing the yellow ones today.

Sometimes the suspicion gets so thick an outsider is tempted to shout, "O.K. I'm a chicken thief! Put me in jail!" It doesn't pay to lie to the locals, however. I can tell you that.

Years ago I ate lunch in a little Idaho town where a semi-truck occupied most of Main Street. When the waitress served my coffee she asked in an off-hand way, "So, what are you doing in town?"

I explained I was interviewing ranchers for a weed control newsletter.

"Oh, and I suppose your next appointment is at two o'clock with Frank Johnson," she said.

"Yes, it is," I said. "But how did you know that?"

"That's my husband," she said.

The best case of outsider profiling I can think of involved three black men who robbed the bank in Near Center, Ohio years ago. (I changed the name of the town to protect the innocent.)

There's no question race played a part in the capture of these fellows. This wasn't racial profiling, however. It was more bad judgment than anything else.

When these men decided to rob that little bank they apparently forgot there were no black people in the community of Near Center — and probably hadn't been in 30 years. They compounded their error by stopping for lunch at the cafe across the street from the bank! (So much for the element of surprise.)

Finally these guys made a cardinal mistake for small town bank robbers. They waited until they got to the bank to put on their masks.

That might work in the city, but it's not the way to do it in a small town. If you plan to rob one of these little banks, you might as well put on your mask before you leave home. They're going to see you coming, anyway.

By the time these fellows got the loot in their car there were road blocks on every highway, side road, and cow path in that end of the county. Racial profiling? Not really.

Extremely poor planning it seems to me.

Over 50

Those who have passed the age of 50 will agree few events change a person's life more than that fateful birthday. We don't feel any older, look any older, or think any differently, but our mail suddenly goes bonkers.

First we get the AARP letters, then new age medicine brochures begin arriving, and finally last week I received an offer for funeral insurance.

Where are these folks getting their lists? I really don't feel all that bad!

The most interesting mail I've received recently is a brochure describing a breakthrough in medical science. This literature explains that scientists once scoffed at medicines and techniques used by the witch doctors, Indian medicine men, and shamans.

But now progressive scientists are recognizing the old tribal doctors had some powerful medicine — and pretty good mailing lists for people over 50. So now all of these folks are in cahoots and sending me brochures nearly twice a week!

My latest medical mailer describes the problem with free

radicals and shows how these particles bounce around our bodies, bombarding cells and upsetting the molecular order. The brochure's authors say the number of cells destroyed by free radicals over the years is enormous.

"Pathologists have found that the size of a 25-year-old person's liver is often twice that of a 70-year-old," they say. (There's some good news. I was afraid it went the other way.)

"As the major organs are eaten away by free radicals, they become less and less efficient, causing many malfunctions within the body."

Here's a photo of a man with skin made of clear plastic. His insides look like the bottom of my tool box: A conglomeration of bolts, springs, and pipe fittings.

The brochure explains that free radicals are oxidants, just like rust is a form of oxidation. We will rust to death inside if we don't take some anti-oxidants. (Or maybe a shot of oil once in awhile.)

I'll skip over the gory details of brain cells exploding, skin wrinkling, and arteries clogging. But, I ask you, is anybody under 50 getting this cheerful information?

The best part of my latest brochure are the letters from satisfied customers. The major theme of these testimonials is that folks are experiencing more energy and an improved sex-drive — although one person reports his golf game has improved by five strokes, also.

One fellow writes, "(This product) has made me feel like I'm 35 years old, not the 55 that I am. My appetite and energy are high, and best of all I'm having sex more than once a night. Here's a big thank you for a sensational product."

I read that and thought, "Who's this guy trying to kid? He may think he's smart now, but he'll be in a heap of trouble when his wife finds out."

Smart Cops

Sometimes it doesn't pay to be too smart. That's the message from New London, Connecticut this week.

News reports say a New London resident took an exam to become a police officer and was not given an interview because he scored too high on the exam. This man filed a federal lawsuit alleging discrimination based on intelligence.

This particular exam is widely used by private companies and hundreds of police departments to determine who's too smart, too dumb, or just right. The New London Chief of Police says candidates who are too smart could get bored with police work and quit soon after completing training.

I should stop here to explain that police departments generally don't discriminate against smart people. But those that do produce some interesting news.

A prime example was described by my brother in Ohio. My brother says his local newspaper reported the sheriff's office was contacted about a case of food tampering.

The caller said she bought a jar of baby food with little, white pills in it. "They looked like aspirin, so I tasted them, and they tasted like aspirin," she said.

A sheriff's deputy hurried out to get the pills. Someone at the sheriff's office tasted them; and sure enough, they were just aspirin.

An even better example was reported in Johannesburg, South Africa recently. Johannesburg police apprehended a burglary suspect who tried to escape by running into the zoo and jumping into the gorilla enclosure. During the ensuing melee:
— The suspect was apprehended by a gorilla named Max
— The suspect shot and wounded Max.
— Max wounded the suspect.
— Police officers entered the enclosure, where they shot and apprehended the burglar.
— Max apprehended two police officers, who suffered minor injuries.
— Then they tranquilized Max and put him in the zoo hospital.

I submit that none of this would have happened if the Johannesburg police had not discriminated against intelligent people. It's easy to imagine what a smart policeman might have done.

First, the smart policeman would notice the burglar jumped into the gorilla enclosure and realize Max was in there, too. A smart cop would not have followed the suspect into the gorilla bin.

He would get on his radio and say, "Alleged suspect is in deep doo-doo. Officer will remain outside gorilla cage as long as necessary. Until retirement, at least."

Then the officer would shout, "Hey, Max. Anybody in there with you? If you can't get out, I'll bet the other guy can't, either."

The policeman would get out a bag of doughnuts and say, "Want a maple bar, Max? You take cream and sugar?"

Pretty soon Max and the burglar would get tired of living together and ask for separate pens. None of this shoot'em-up, mix-it-up with the gorilla stuff.

That's what we need in law enforcement, as far as I'm concerned. People who can stop and think.

Stick To Your Guns

The wars in Kosovo and other Balkan states should remind us of the freedoms we enjoy in this country. It's easy to forget our liberties hinge upon interpretation of the Constitution, rather than the whims of Congress, the President, or local politicians.

I find that comforting. Those who believe the framers of our Constitution were lacking in foresight should remember the Serbian people trusted their political leaders at least as much as we do ours.

Many of the things that happened in Kosovo could not happen here. That's because many folks in the U.S. own guns, one of those freedoms granted by the Constitution.

If three masked men appeared in my backyard and ordered me to move out (reportedly common in Kosovo), I'm almost sure I could get two of them. I'd feel real bad if I didn't get all three.

Some folks think guns are a bad thing, regardless of what the Constitution says. They believe the police and the government can take care of us.

Others believe there's no reason for people to own certain kinds of firearms. They say a gun shouldn't be capable of firing more than 10 rounds before reloading, for example. Some say four shots is plenty. Others think zero is about right. A lot of people see no need for handguns, especially inexpensive ones. If we outlaw inexpensive guns, maybe fewer people will buy them? (The crooks will keep on stealing them, however.)

Some believe a waiting period should be required to buy a gun, as well as a background check. Maybe finger printing. Dealers should be required to sell a trigger lock with each firearm.

Many think no one under 21 should have a handgun, or possibly any gun. They believe folks should be required to keep firearms locked-up, take a proficiency test, and have firearms registered so the police know who has what.

Once in awhile someone will stop and ask, "Do any of these laws do any good?" The answer is generally, "No, but we have to do something."

I used to think the National Rifle Association was alarmist when that organization suggests each of these laws are just a crack in the dike for those who believe people shouldn't be allowed to own guns. I've changed my mind, however. (Congressman Schumer wouldn't do something like that, would he?)

The major excuse for many new laws is keeping guns away from kids. How are we going to do that? We can't keep anything else away from them.

We tend to forget guns have done kids a lot more good than harm. Millions of kids have developed a lifelong hobby as hunters or target shooters. These kids generally get into much less trouble than those without such interests.

Our schools teach drivers' training, drug prevention, and sex education, but most won't even consider gun safety classes. Teachers, parents, and administrators fear gun safety instruction might kindle kids' interest in firearms.

So, what's wrong with that? Pattern it after sex education. The school nurse could hand out some trigger locks.

The Outhouse Was Cheaper

A recent piece in the travel news reminded me of how much we take for granted. The news report says the Four Seasons Hotel in Washington D.C. has installed a new Quiet Room in the hotel fitness center that can be rented for $30 per hour.

The Quiet Room is a "soundproof, dimly lit, securely locked 10-by-12 foot space furnished only with a leather massage recliner, an audio/visual system to pipe in the sounds of waves, forest noises or bird calls, and a small refrigerator. That's it," the story says.

The point of such a room is quiet and solitude. "No phones. No interruptions. And no couples."

Can you imagine the desk clerk asking folks like me if we want to rent the quiet room for $30 an hour? "Oh, heck no! The noisiest room you've got will be fine for me."

It's hard for most of us to imagine getting so stressed out we would pay $30 an hour for some peace and quiet. Many readers will recall we got all of that for free when everybody had an outhouse.

The outhouse was our quiet room when I was a kid. No

phones. No fax. And no interruptions. (You hoped.)

Nobody ever spent an hour in the outhouse, of course; unless they had chores to do or were hiding from someone.

The old outhouses had just about everything the Four Seasons Quiet Room has. The walls were thin, so forest noises and bird calls were never far away.

If your privy was near a creek (as many were), there was the sound of mountain water in the background. When the sound of water increased we knew the creek was coming up and quiet time should be coming to a close.

We had farm noises, too. There were cows mooing, roosters crowing, and tractors starting up.

I don't know if the Four Seasons has those sounds in their Quiet Room, but they should have. It would make a lot of folks feel right at home.

Some of the world's great decisions were made in an outhouse. That's where Abe Lincoln decided to run for President, Teddy Roosevelt drew maps of the national parks, and General MacArthur vowed he might return if he ever got the chance.

All that changed when health departments started making folks put their bathrooms in the house. Now we've got people spending $30 an hour looking for some peace and quiet!

Nowadays, the majority of the population wouldn't know an outhouse from a tool shed. I don't know what folks would pay for the privilege of sitting in an outhouse, but $30 an hour might be stretching it a little.

Sometimes when I hear folks griping about global warming, methane gas, and environmental degradation, I wonder if they ever saw an outhouse. A couple of hours in one of those little buildings would surely make the outside world look a whole lot better.

Spotted Hotwings

This has been a good year for disasters: Drought, floods, snow, hurricanes, you name it. Anyone who hasn't had a disaster this year is certainly entitled to some kind of award.

Nearly every day we see the President flying around the country looking at disasters. Then he comes on the news and explains how he's going to help everyone affected by this unprecedented event.

I don't think I've ever seen a more generous person than our President. That man must have a lot of money.

I'm in favor of disaster relief, of course, but I think the federal government has gotten a little carried away with the whole thing.

I remember when Mount St. Helens blew her top in the early '80's. I was a county extension agent about 100 miles from St. Helens, and the mountain report soon became the news of the day.

The bigwigs in Washington D.C. would call up Washington State University and ask, "What's the mountain doing today?"

The university guys would say solemnly, "It looks pretty calm now, but we know it could go off at any time. We're just taking it day by day."

Readers may recall that Mount St. Helens was spewing small amounts of volcanic ash for months after the initial eruption. These little burps of dust would drift north, south, east, or west, depending upon the wind of the day.

One evening I got a call from a university administrator. "We just heard that Mount St. Helens erupted again today," he said.

"How does it look in your area? I was wondering, is there anything we should do?"

This hit me crosswise for some reason. The mountain is erupting. What should Washington State University and cooperative extension do?

All I could think of was, "Unless we've got an awfully big cork, I can't see us doing much of anything."

A few weeks ago I read that someone found a county in the state of Washington that didn't have a disaster this year. Wahkiakum County (in the southwest corner of the state) was forced to refuse federal relief because they couldn't find a disaster.

Folks were so startled they didn't know what to do. Every other county in Washington is getting some kind of relief for natural disasters.

Wahkiakum County might still qualify, though. This week I learned that wildlife agents raided the tavern in Skamokawa, Washington (Wahkiakum County) to rescue an owl.

It seems researchers in Oregon tagged a few spotted owls and were following them around with a radio antennae when one of the little boogers stopped beeping. The researchers finally crossed the Columbia River and picked up the owl's signal at the tavern in Skamokawa.

Suspecting the worst (spotted hotwings), law enforcement agents swooped down on the tavern. They found an electronic dart board giving off signals like an owl with a radio transmitter on his back.

Does that qualify as a disaster? It does if you're a wildlife agent in Skamokawa.

A Tough Sell

I don't know about you, but I'm tired of sales calls. I don't mind calls from folks I do business with; but those guys who go through the phone book, calling up everyone, are a pain in the neck.

Some of my favorites are the hearing-aid companies. They want to give me a hearing test. "Our representative will be in your area next week and would be happy to stop by for a free hearing examination," they say.

"What? You'll have to speak up," I tell them. "I can't hear a word you're saying."

"We want to check your hearing!" the caller shouts.

"No, my paint isn't smearing. We just got new siding and the roof is fine, too."

Then, I hang up. "That should stop them for awhile," I surmise. Who do they think they're kidding, calling-up folks and suggesting hearing exams?

If they want to give hearing exams, they should be sending letters. If they want to give eye exams; then call us on the phone. You can't call a deaf person and set up an appointment!

I figure the hearing-aid people are trying to sell us something we don't need. That's why nobody calls to offer eye exams. (They send letters for those.)

Can you imagine this guy coming to my house to check my hearing? He probably has some fancy equipment — or a watch that doesn't tick, to convince me I need a hearing-aid.

These telemarketers remind me of the old-time vacuum sweeper salesmen — the ones who would throw dirt all over your rug, and then try to prove how good their vacuum was.

The old-fashioned salesmen had to watch their step, though. Readers may have heard about the young sweeper salesman who arrived at a remote farmhouse with his vacuum and a bag of shop-sweepings.

This place was way out in the boonies, but the lady of the house let him in, anyway. Peddlers were just part of the environment in those days, and a sweeper salesman was kind of a novelty.

"Our vacuum is guaranteed to out-perform anything you have ever used or you get your money back," the salesman began. "This is our top-of-the-line, commercial model, with 14 attachments and the extra long cord."

Then, he tossed his bag of dirt on the cream-colored carpet, and proceeded to unravel his sweeper cord.

"Don't you worry about your carpet for one minute," he said, searching for an electrical outlet. "If this vacuum doesn't clean this dirt up in less than 30 seconds. I'll lick it up myself."

"Well, I sure hope you skipped breakfast," the woman said. "Cause we're four miles from electricity, and that's a brand new rug you'll be eating off of."

Tourist Farming

It's easy to forget how much agriculture has changed over the years. My generation has seen the days of two-row corn planters and the era of precision agriculture with satellite technology.

One thing hasn't changed, though: The competitive nature of farming. Everyone is looking for crops, livestock, and enterprises that will help improve the bottom line.

A few farmers are taking their cues from the tourist business by providing farm activities for city people. These entrepreneurs have discovered baling hay, building fence, and milking cows are great entertainment for folks who never had to do them.

It's hard to believe people will pay good money to do things their grandparents spent most of their lives trying to avoid, but that's the way it is. Some farmers are planting entire fields of corn and cutting them into mazes so tourists can wander around, wondering how they are going to get out.

I can't imagine anybody getting lost in a cornfield on purpose. The whole thing seems terribly embarrassing to me.

Tourist farming (or agri-tourism) may sound strange at first, but it's a natural progression in many ways. Folks who grew up on a farm have been dealing with tourists for most of their lives. We called them "town kids" when I was a boy.

Getting lost in the cornfield was a minor event compared to the stunts we pulled on the town kids. Most of our pranks were harmless — even educational in a warped sort of way.

My friend Jim's brown cow trick was one of my favorites. Jim's family had a few cows and an excellent pasture for baseball, so he always kept a few town kids around for the weekend baseball games.

Most Saturdays we would play baseball until about 5:00 P.M., and then we had to quit so Jim could milk the cows. While Jim gathered the cows, I generally mixed-up some powdered milk-replacer for the calves.

One company made a chocolate colored milk-replacer in those days, and that's what Jim had for his calves.

Everyone knows the old story about brown cows giving chocolate milk. So we'd mix up a batch of chocolate milk-replacer and try to convince the town kids we got it from the old black cow in the last stanchion.

Our friends were skeptical at first, but they always came around. Seeing is believing, I guess.

When I read about agri-tourism, bed and breakfasts, and cornfield mazes, I always remember those days when the town kids came to the farm to visit. That's the main reason I could never run an agri-tourist business.

I'd have to stop every so often and say, "Wait a minute! These folks are paying to swing on the hay rope. Maybe we'd better actually tie it to something this time?"

Who Was That Masked Animal

Some days I wonder what this world is coming to. Our society has become so urbanized we are forced to rely upon television, books, and newspapers for most of our information about animals.

As a result, we have become fair game for all sorts of myths about wild and domestic animals. The news media does what it can to defend the critters, but the complete story is often lacking.

A reporter will write, "Joe Blow was attacked by a bear as he walked to his outhouse last week. Wildlife officers were forced to destroy the bear, even though Mr. Blow built his outhouse in the bear's natural habitat."

Folks seem to forget Joe Blow has lived there 30 years, and the bear was only three years old. There's no way this critter could be holding a grudge.

In an effort to be fair, I am going to a print a few letters about animals and answer some of the questions most folks would be afraid to ask.

Dear Mr. Pond:

We recently moved to the country and bought some sheep. There are lots of coyotes around, and I've read some coyotes will kill sheep if there aren't enough rodents around, or the weather is bad, or the individual coyote is mad about something. Is this true?

Signed,
Sheepish

Dear Sheepish:

I am happy you mentioned that "some coyotes" will kill sheep. We must constantly remind ourselves we are not talking about all coyotes. Only bad coyotes do this sort of thing.

Several things can cause a coyote to go bad. First he must be big enough to be bad. If the coyote is too small the sheep will just laugh at him.

This becomes part of the problem when the little coyotes grow up. There would be more sheep alive today if they hadn't laughed at the little coyotes.

The best thing a sheep owner can do is teach her sheep to remain as serious as possible. This isn't easy, as sheep seem to be born with a smirk on their face.

Dear Mr. Pond:

I recently noticed a furry, little animal visiting the chicken house and gathering eggs nearly every day. This animal has brown fur, black rings around it's tail, and looks to be wearing a mask.

My husband says it's a raccoon. What do you think?

Signed,
Ms. Demeggs

Dear Ms. Demeggs:

Your husband might be right, but let's not be too hasty. The animal you describe could be a groundhog in a Lone Ranger costume. It takes a trained biologist to distinguish one of these from a raccoon.

I tend to think the raccoon is not a true species at all, but just a bunch of woodchucks looking for a party.

Yard Sale

Can you believe it? Here we are on a two-day fishing trip, while the wives are back home having a yard sale.

Is that frightening, or what?! The only thing that scares me worse than a yard sale is a house remodeling. Being away from home during either one is just asking for trouble.

We figured the fishing equipment was safe. We had most of that with us. But who knows what else might go on the block?

Before we left I told my wife, "You can sell anything you want, as long as it isn't mine."

I knew I could trust her on this one. That's one thing we have in common: We're just not yard sale people. Connie likes to buy at yard sales, but she's never been on the selling end before.

It takes a certain psychology to have a yard sale. You've got to say, "O.K., I don't need this stuff, and I might as well sell it."

As opposed to, "Wait a minute. I might need that again someday."

Or, "You can't sell that! That's the diorama I made in sixth grade, depicting the Pilgrims crashing into Plymouth Rock."

That's my problem — I never seem to have anything I can part with. Things I haven't seen or used in 20 years still have value for me.

My old gun rack hasn't been used for years, but it will work great for fishing rods — when I find a wall to put it on. Those old sinks in the barn might never be sinks again, but they'll make fine grain feeders if we decide to get some livestock.

Just last week I wanted to put my 40-year-old telescope on a new .22 rifle, but I couldn't find mounts that would fit the old scope and the new rifle.

My son said he had a BB gun scope with the right size mounts many years ago. The scope was broken, so he threw it away.

"You threw it away?!" I exclaimed. "How could you do that? I've never thrown anything away!"

It's easier for me to get rid of things if someone else bought them in the first place. It takes me a long time to buy something, and I'll be darned if I'm going to admit that I didn't need it.

That's why you find so many gifts at yard sales. If it weren't for gifts, yard sales would dry up and blow away.

Everyone has a few obvious candidates, though. Clothes that no longer fit are a good example.

When I have clothes that are too big, I'm happy to sell them. Anything that's too small goes to the dump. (I'll be darned if I'm going to admit I've outgrown my clothes.)

Clothes that have gone out of style would seem a natural choice, but what if they come back in? You just never know. My clothes have been in and out of style four of five times over the years.

I think everyone understands the best items for a yard sale are stuff that belongs to your spouse. That's why nobody in his right mind would go fishing when there's a yard sale going on!

Gourmet Lunches

"Ah, here's one," I thought. "This might be lunch, or maybe a snack?"

Actually, I can't tell what it is. It's one of those meals I packed months ago.

I find them in my hunting coat, in the glove box, and under the boat seat. Some are dry and chewy looking. The majority are green and hard to identify.

Some of these meals are partially eaten. Others haven't been touched; apparently judged too bad to eat, but too good to throw away.

My son says the Army has some food they call MRE's, "Meals Ready to Eat." He claims they are pretty good.

The food in my coat pocket could be called SIF's, "Stuff I Found." It might have been good when I packed it, but it's pretty bad when I find it weeks later. If I packed better lunches to begin with, I probably wouldn't find so many leftovers.

There's an art to packing a lunch. One can't just throw a baloney sandwich in a bag and expect it to look appetizing at lunch time.

The best lunches I can remember belonged to my old friend, Steve. Steve's lunch always featured a main course and at least four side dishes.

He would have fried chicken, ham and cheese on sourdough, pork tenderloin wrapped in a dinner roll, gourmet potato chips (with dip), two kinds of pickles, smoked salmon for a snack, and chocolate pudding for dessert.

Nobody ever found one of Steve's lunches ripening under a boat seat. He ate every bit of them.

One day I was marveling at Steve's lunch and questioning how he got his wife to pack it, when I recalled a story by the late Gene Hill. Hill's story describes his friend who always showed up with a beautiful lunch and all of the garnishments.

Hill's hunting buddy wouldn't think of venturing into the field without a perfectly packed lunch and a little glass of wine to go with it.

"That's the only thing missing," I told Steve. "Your wife packs a nice lunch, but she forgot the wine. I guess it's pretty hard to carry a glass of wine when you're chukar hunting."

A couple of weeks later, my friend and I were climbing along the same ridge, hunting the same chukars, when we decided to stop for lunch. Steve stifled a grin as he unpacked his fried chicken, pickles, potato chips, a little cheese roll (with crackers), and a cupcake for dessert.

Then, he pulled out two wine glasses, and one of those little bottles like they serve in expensive restaurants. Next, he fished out his cork screw and said, "I'm sorry we don't have a better selection of wines today.

"I just wasn't sure what would go with your baloney sandwich."

Christmas Letter

I finally did it. I wrote a Christmas letter.

I wrote my letter before Christmas — even though you will be reading this after the holiday. Lots of folks read my Christmas letter after the holidays, but I blame that on the postal service. (I started writing in plenty of time.)

Besides, Christmas letters are like fruitcakes. They're not going to spoil.

I've never sent a Christmas letter before, in deference to folks who think these missives are stilted and impersonal. I suppose they could be, but almost any news is better than no news.

I admit there's something about recounting the year's events that makes a person giddy. There's nothing like four pages of vacation stories or the minute details of Junior's first birthday to keep the reader on the edge of his chair.

Even that wouldn't be so bad if they didn't list the ingredients in the baby's cake. He wouldn't have spit-up if they hadn't used so much chocolate.

My Christmas letter was nothing like that. Anyone who

enjoys two pages of fishing stories probably got a big kick out of it.

We've sent family photos with our Christmas cards for years, but we forgot to do that this time. Maybe it was just too big of a project.

Last year we sent photos of my wife and me with the kids. The year before our pictures included Connie and me, plus the kids and their dogs.

Family photos are nice, but they're such a hassle. How can you get a picture of everyone and still find someone to operate the camera?

I solved that problem last year with that little timer on the camera. The one that gives you twenty seconds to run into the photo, adjust your tie, and bare your teeth.

We got everyone lined up on the hearth in front of the fireplace and set the camera on a tripod. The kids were sitting in front, Connie was in the middle, and I was supposed to squat down on the hearth behind them.

I've taken these before, so I'm kind of an expert at it. I focused the camera, made sure the flash was working, and set the timer.

Then, I ran to the hearth, squeezed-in behind everyone and squatted down. The camera went off, and everyone was smiling — except me.

The kids said I should have noticed the fireplace poker before I set the timer, but I can't see how that was my fault. I never take a good photo, anyway.

Well, I got my Christmas letter mailed, and I hope everyone had a nice holiday. If you didn't get my letter, drop me a note and I'll send you one.

If you didn't get a photo, forget it. I'm not taking any more of those.

Tire Tracks On The Mail

I got my birthday card today. Every few years the Department of Licensing sends me a cute, little card saying, "We'd like to wish you a Happy Birthday and remind you of the expiration of your driver's license."

How nice of them to think of me! Who says public employees aren't nice to people?

I remember a time I didn't get my reminder (or lost it) and my license expired, unbeknownst to me. I was renting a car more than 2,000 miles from home, when the guy behind the desk asked to see my driver's license.

He looked at my license and said, "Do you have a current license? This one is expired."

"That's impossible!" I thought. "My birthday was six months ago, and I'm not the kind of person who drives around without a driver's license!"

But there it was, expired; and I was supposed to pick up my nephew in a hour to play golf. My brother-in-law had to take me to his house to pick up my wife so she could rent the car.

There I was with a rented car, an expired driver's license,

and a golf appointment in 30 minutes. "Big deal!?" some folks would say. "You've been driving without a license for six months. What's a few more days?"

That's what I thought, too. So we drove around the block, switched drivers, and I arrived at the first tee — right on time.

That's not the point of my story, though. My point is the woman at the Department of Licensing was nice as could be when I got back home.

She didn't ask how I forgot to renew, eschewed comments about older people making notes, and was just very helpful. There were several folks in the office, and she was nice to everyone. That's pretty much normal in a small town, I think, despite the bad press public employees have to endure.

We could take the local post office for another example. Everyone in our post office does a great job, as far as I'm concerned; and they're always friendly. Even when people don't deserve it, they're friendly.

Postal employees take so much flak, I wondered what would happen if I accused them of being nice. I finally got my chance when we started getting shipping receipts with happy faces on the envelopes.

These aren't real mail, subject to 50,000 pages of federal regulations, so happy faces are O.K. But I complained to the postmaster.

"Marty," I said. "I've got a complaint. Someone has been drawing happy faces on my receipt envelopes. I figured it wasn't you, but I've always heard postal employees aren't supposed to be friendly."

"You bet it wasn't me," he said. "If it was me, it would have been tire tracks."

Movie House

The Federal Trade Commission (FTC) and our political leaders are aghast at a study showing the entertainment industry targets youth with violent and sexually explicit programming. The FTC is apparently not very smart. Everyone else has known this since television was invented.

Defenders of the industry suggest this is not their problem. They say parents should monitor their kids' television watching, movies, video games, internet access, magazines, books, and the air they breathe.

The folks who suggest parental supervision for nearly everything are the same ones who believe schools should provide breakfast, lunch, and dinner for the students. They say many parents don't have the time, knowledge, and skills to offer these things at home.

If parents don't have time for meals, how can we expect them to monitor everything else the child does?

There's no question our society has a problem here. I can't prove things were better when I was a kid, but we surely didn't get the confusing signals kids receive today. When our theater advertised an "off-color" movie everyone knew that meant it was in black and white.

Our movie house showed the old westerns and an occasional horror film, but nothing anyone would object to. The theater was filled with kids on Saturday night, and Jane, the proprietor, was like a mother to all of us. Her kids were there too; so she was a mother to some of us.

I can't remember ever seeing an adult in that theater. That's understandable, I guess.

The most offensive thing about the movies we watched was the audience itself. Anything that could be considered funny on the screen was immediately transformed into a full-scale riot by the audience.

Each kid had his own laugh in those days, and everyone was looking for something to heehaw about. The slightest snicker would launch the crowd into a uproar that would do a flock of peacocks proud.

We had to be careful, though. Anyone who got too rowdy was subject to expulsion. Being tossed out of the theater was not something we wanted on our resume'.

The best laugh belonged to my friend, Jim. His laugh reminded one of a huge donkey, beginning as a small "heeaw" and progressing into a raucous "Heeaw — Heeaaw — HEEAAAW! — HEEAAAW! — HEEAAAW!"

Jim's laugh was perfected over the years and was good for nearly any movie, "B" westerns, horror flicks, or documentaries. He saved it for the most opportune times.

One instance I can remember Jim launching his laugh was during a cartoon featuring a huge bear. The bear was wearing bib overalls and an old, floppy hat. (What was that bear's name?)

The bear's pants were much too large and dragged along the ground behind, giving him the appearance of a baby who needed his diaper changed. Jim commented to this effect and cut loose with his famed "Heeaw — Heeaw — HEEAAAW! — HEEAAAW! — HEEAAAW!"

Jane threatened to throw us out. But we were back the next Saturday.

Home Office

A recent news report suggests folks who work at home should adopt a "who cares" attitude about background noise filtering into the office. The writer says callers don't care if we work at home as long as the noise isn't disruptive.

She quotes a man who used to lock the kids out of his office and forbid his wife from practicing her bassoon during business hours. Now he leaves the office door open and his wife does whatever she pleases.

This fellow has decided business callers don't worry about background noise as long as it doesn't interrupt their call.

That may be fine for him, but it wouldn't work for me. My callers would be shocked if I said, "I'll have to call you back as soon as my wife gets off her bassoon."

Anyone lucky enough to have an office in the house should be thankful for it. I used to work out of my barn and that wasn't any picnic, either.

My barn office was upstairs — above the sheep and the chickens. I don't know what callers thought, but the critters could get pretty unruly sometimes.

Spring was the worst time to call me in those days. That's when we weaned the lambs and the noise was overwhelming for a couple of days.

The kids had their 4-H lambs downstairs most of the summer, and these animals had a habit of injecting a "Baa!" into a conversation at the worst of times. A client would suggest an amount they would be willing to pay for my column, and the sheep would say, "Baa!"

We kept some chickens on the lower level, too. Many times I would pause during a telephone conversation to explain what was going on down there.

The hens would get to cackling, and I would say, "Sounds like the girls are having a time downstairs. Must be another birthday."

The big critters weren't the worst of it, either. My barn office was a haven for tree frogs and several kinds of insects.

I would pick up a phone book and find a dried frog under it, or turn on the computer and a bug would come walking out of the "B" drive. All of these creatures thought they knew more about writing than I did, and unfortunately they might have been right.

The worst thing about a barn office or a home office is the tendency to use it for things other than business. Things like cutting up venison, weighing fish on the postal scales, or shearing sheep.

The UPS people must have been surprised to walk into my office each fall and find me whacking away on the front half of a deer. They took it all in stride, though. UPS gives them special training on keeping a straight face.

I moved my office into the house years ago. Now I work in the basement, next to the bathroom.

The only background noise I worry about is my wife taking a shower. "And please don't flush the toilet!"

God Bless The Hatcheries

"You got him!" My son shouted. The fish came at the boat, under the boat, and around the front.

"He's headed for the anchor!" I groaned. The fish turns back under the boat and ripps out some line. I thrust the rod tip under water to work the line away from the motor and out the other side.

The fish takes more line and turns again. Then it shoots under the boat, and swirls 20 yards out the opposite side. I'm holding the rod tip under water and hoping for the best.

Finally, I get this critter on my side of the boat and Russ nets it: The prettiest 10 lb steelhead I have ever seen.

Must have been a wild fish? Nope, it's one of those inferior hatchery steelhead we've been reading about. Inferior to what? I have to wonder.

We can tell this is a hatchery fish because the adipose fin has been clipped. Nobody can tell from the fight.

Later that morning, my son hooked a steelhead of about 7 lb. I barely had my line out of the water when this fish was next to the boat and ready for landing.

Must have been a hatchery fish? Nope, this was a wild steelhead — according to the intact adipose fin.

Russ credits his superior rod handling ability for the short fight, but I've heard that one before.

Same place a year ago. My son caught a steelhead that was barely four pounds. The same day I caught one four times that big, and his fought harder than mine!

Which was the hatchery fish? They both were.

This is no fluke. Anyone who can tell hatchery steelhead from wild steelhead on a hook and line is going to have to prove it to me.

I'm told biologists agree that hatchery steelhead are inferior to wild fish. Maybe we should survey the biologists again?

I recall a farmer friend who called several years ago to say he was tired of listening to certain groups and their pseudo scientists. "Their base of information seems to be 'everybody knows'," he said.

Of course a steelhead or salmon can't be measured by how it fights on the end of a line. There are other tests of superiority: Such as the ability to migrate to the ocean, return to the place of birth, and reproduce after they get there.

Idaho's sockeye salmon might be a good example. An Associated Press story reports the Idaho Department of Fish and Game counted 257 sockeye returning to Idaho this year (2000), surpassing biologists predictions of 100 fish.

That's not a large number, but returns of Idaho sockeye in the 1990's were in the single digits, some years as low as one, or zero. Biologists collected eggs from the few remaining sockeye and ran them through a hatchery (heaven forbid).

The AP story quotes Idaho's manager of sockeye programs, Paul Kline. "This validates our supposition that we would not lose species productivity by taking the wild population into the hatchery.

"Sockeye returns were good enough this year to cause me to believe they have a good chance of rebounding when survival conditions improve."

What if some of these hatchery sockeye mate with fish that were spawned in the river? I, for one, wish them all the happiness in the world.

Minivan?!

Here's another attempt to insinuate that SUV buyers are a bunch of nut cases. Minivan buyers, on the other hand, are about the nicest people you would ever want to meet.

A story from the New York Times News Service says automakers have learned these things from closely guarded psychological research. The story claims buyers of sports utility vehicles are "more restless, more sybaritic, less social people who have strong conscious and subconscious fears of crime."

Minivan owners, on the other hand, are more self-confident and more "other oriented" — more involved with family, friends, and communities. Folks like me, who own an SUV and an old pickup truck, should probably be fitted with a jacket that buttons up the back.

I feel sorry for people who own both a minivan and an SUV. They must be terribly confused.

I don't know where the media is getting this stuff. Anyone who uses the word "sybaritic" scares the devil out of me, anyway.

I can't speak for other SUV owners, but I need mine to

pull my boat. Every time I see a guy pulling a boat with a minivan I think to myself, "That poor devil is so hen-pecked his wife won't even let him use the truck."

Automakers think we have deeper psychological reasons for buying SUVs. The New York Times story quotes David P. Bostwick, DaimlerChrysler's director of market research as saying minivan buyers tend to be more comfortable than sport utility buyers with being married.

"We have a basic resistance in our society to admitting we are parents, and no longer able to go out and find another mate," Bostwick says. "If you have a sport utility, you can have the smoked windows, put the children in the back and pretend you are still single."

Are you kidding me? Pretend you are single with a back seat full of kids?!

My kids are grown up, but I wouldn't mind having the smoked windows. They would hide the sheep if nothing else.

Bostwick seems to have an obsession with this marriage thing. He says sport utility buyers are more commonly concerned about feeling sexy, and like the idea they could use their vehicles to start dating again.

There's one good way to put the kibosh on that kind of thinking. My brother heard this on the Red Green show.

Red always has a little segment where he talks to the "older fellas," as he calls them. "You know who you are," he says.

"I know some of you fellas have a little squabble with the missus now and then," Red says. "Sometimes you might get to thinking a divorce would be a good idea.

"Here's what you should do when that happens. Just go into the bathroom and take off all your clothes.

"Then look in the mirror. Turn around. Take a good look," he continues.

"Now, do you really think you're in dating shape? Maybe you'd better just get back in there and try to patch things up."

Don't Laugh At The Stooges

Here's one for further study. A report from Knight Ridder News Service says two Toronto psychologists have located a segment of the brain responsible for a person's sense of humor.

These psychologists observed 31 men and women to determine how each responded to jokes. Some of the participants in the study had minor brain damage while others did not.

The researchers found brain damage in general didn't curtail a person's sense of humor, but those with damage to the brain's right frontal lobe had trouble with certain types of jokes. The scientists said these persons appreciated only obvious, slapstick humor.

I'm O.K. with that. I've long suspected aberrations in the brain play a role in certain types of humor. That's how we get TV sitcoms.

I have trouble with certain kinds of jokes, too. But that doesn't keep me from telling them.

Earlier studies also suggest the right side of the brain is the lightning rod for humor. Subjects in these studies wore caps to measure brain waves while they were subjected to jokes.

A few patients, who burst into spontaneous giggling for no apparent reason, were thought to have tumors on the right frontal lobe of the brain.

I'm not a scientist, but I'd take another look at those wired-up caps before I started diagnosing brain tumors. Any kid who's ever been to church can tell us spontaneous giggling and hats often go together.

My problem with the Toronto study is the researchers' incessant probing into the anatomy of humor. These psychologists say the simple, slapstick humor enjoyed by folks with frontal lobe damage is similar to jokes "appreciated by young children and men."

That leads the scientists (laughing and giggling) down the slippery slope of gender differences. They claim earlier studies show women enjoy jokes that are more complicated — sophisticated if you will, while men and young children prefer slapstick, "such as the Three Stooges."

I can't speak for other men, but that's not a bit funny in my opinion. What's wrong with the Three Stooges, anyway? I think they're pretty funny!

Besides, humor isn't a matter of sophistication. It's a matter of experience.

Women see one Stooge hit another with a two-by-four and think that's the dumbest thing they ever saw. Men see the same thing and remember helping the neighbor build his new deck.

Women watch Moe crank his old Model T and wonder, "Why is Larry holding onto the spark plug wire with one hand and Curley's ear with the other?" Men see the same thing and remember their high school shop teacher.

Women think the Three Stooges are just a bunch of clumsy bozos. Men see them as a parody on the human condition.

A Flock Of Fishermen

The sport of fishing has certainly changed over the years. Gone are the days when a person could walk into the hardware store and buy his whole outfit for $20.

One thing hasn't changed, though. Fishermen are as gregarious as ever. Much like sheep, I think.

I don't mean to seem anti-social or anything like that, but I prefer to fish with my companions; not with every fisherman on the lake. That's why I cringe at the frequent suggestion from outdoor writers, "If you don't know where to fish, just follow the other boats." Or the equivalent advice, "Ask a lot of questions."

I enjoy fishing, but I hate questions. Sometimes I want to ask, "Is this some kind of survey, or what?" A recent trip to the river is a case in point.

My son and I launched our boat and headed for our favorite spot. We passed one boat on the way, then motored on down the river another 400 yards.

We circled around like a dog looking for a place to lie down and dropped the anchor. Before we could bait-up, the fishermen in the other boat pulled anchor, ran up beside us, and set up 20 yards away.

Why would they do that? Our spot wasn't any better than theirs, and they had miles of water to choose from.

It happens all the time. My boat is old, and my equipment looks like the final day of a yard sale, but fishermen follow us around.

Apparently they think, "Hey, those guys can't afford nice equipment. They must spend a lot of time fishing."

My brother and I had a similar experience on the coast a few years ago. We launched our boat about 8:00 A.M. and motored out into the bay.

I was surprised to see most of the boats were concentrated further back in the bay than I observed on a previous trip. Maybe the fish had moved? This is a large body of water, and 100 boats can scatter out very well if they want to.

I'm pretty stubborn, though. So we fished where I caught fish two weeks before. The results were meager.

The next day our boat was the first one out, so we headed for the spot we fished the day before. (Did I tell you I'm kind of stubborn?)

Pretty soon boats began arriving and dropping anchors all around us. That's when we realized everybody was following everybody else. The first boat out determines where everyone fishes.

Two old guys putted up in their little pram and asked, "Doing any good?"

"Nope," we told them. They motored over to the next boat and asked, "Doing any good?"

Those folks said, "Nope," and the old-timers moved off a few yards and dropped their anchor.

We left soon after that and decided to try a spot where there weren't any boats — about a half mile away. Pretty soon the two old boys in the little boat came chugging by.

"You fellas doin' any good up here?" they asked.

"Nope," we said. So they moved off about thirty feet and tossed out their anchor!

Return Of The Frogs

Every so often I have to confess I never took a class in journalism. I don't know why I need to confess, it's pretty obvious to anyone who knows anything about journalism.

It's like the old minister said, "Don't be too quick to confess your sins; if you're that bad everyone already knows about it."

My lack of training explains my difficulty writing good leads for stories. The famous writer, James Thurber, described a similar defect in a classmate of his.

Thurber's classmate, an agriculture student, had a terrible time coming up with anything interesting to write about. In desperation, his journalism professor sent him over to the university horse barns to dig something up.

The professor's instructions were, "This university owns more horses than any other school in the Big Ten. Now get over there and find something interesting — and I want to see a catchy lead this time!"

The ag student did as he was told. He soon returned with a hot story about a disease that was causing blisters on the backs of horses in the university herd. His story began, "Has anybody noticed the horses' backs lately?"

So what's wrong with that? It reminds me of the frogs around my house. Has anybody noticed there's a ton of frogs around my house?

It seems a person can hardly pick up a magazine or newspaper these days without reading about the demise of the frogs. They're going extinct, growing extra legs, jumping sideways.

Somebody needs to tell my frogs they're going extinct. These frogs are reproducing like crazy, crawling under everything, and jumping straight up and down — just like they always have.

My frogs have all of their appendages, too. That's because they're little, bitty tree frogs. If they were big, fat bull frogs this might be a whole different story.

I've always considered it a mistake to get too sentimental about frogs, anyway. If they want to croak, they croak. They're like sheep in that respect.

I suppose the magazine articles are about particular species of frogs, but there must be similarities between these creatures. Biologists blame ultra-violet light, pesticides, and global warming for frailty in frogs.

We have all of those things where I live, but we've got frogs coming out our ears. I counted two on the outdoor faucet, one in the flower boxes, two in a carton of pop, two in the dog's water dish, and several more hiding in the door frames.

If that's going extinct, I'd be real worried if the population recovers.

Computer Breakdown

I finally broke down and bought a new computer. That's the way it works with computers: You either break down and buy a new one, or your computer breaks down — and then you buy one.

I've put this off for quite awhile. All this talk about the world shutting down next January made me think I'd better have at least one computer that works.

I suppose everyone remembers the Y2K bug. That's the problem created by computer geeks who decided computer chips should read years as two digits instead of four. That way, the year 2,000 might be read as 1900, 1800, or 5,000 B.C.

This saves some space on computer chips, but now it's costing business and government billions to correct that little glitch. Some folks think computer experts were kind of dumb to pull a trick like that, but I'm not so sure. Imagine how many folks found jobs working on the Y2K problem.

My new computer is immune to bugs, though. It runs on Microsoft Windows.

You can't buy a new computer that doesn't run on Windows or the Apple equivalent. Some folks think that's a monopoly, but Microsoft says it's just a coincidence.

Everybody has to use a mouse to run Windows. I hate mice. My typing teacher hated mice, too, and she'd kick over her old Underwood if she knew how kids are being taught today.

Experts say the time is coming when we will do everything with our mouse (mice, meece). Typing will be outmoded and spelling will be unnecessary. A person will just use his mouse to pick out a word, and the computer will insert that word into a sentence.

Even now some computers will work from voice commands. If I had one of those I could talk into it and the computer would write, "Ah woke up this mornin' cuz Ma Dog was narcing like bad."

The trend in computers is to design them to do everything.

My daughter got a new computer last week. She called and asked, "Can you hear me?"

"Well, I can hear you to some extent, but not very well," I replied.

"I'll get a little closer to the microphone," she said. "This is so cool. I'm talking to you through my computer!"

"Amazing!" I said. "That should be handy when you can't find your phone."

My new computer has all the bells and whistles. I can't write with it yet, but it whistles and dings like nobody's business. My wife says this new technology lets me access the internet, download information, and send e-mail to friends.

I don't think I'll ever send e-mail to friends. Even if I had friends, I don't think I'd send them e-mail.

Folks who've been getting no mail all these years might go into shock if they started finding it on their computer.

Who Says I'm Lost?

If a man lost his mind, would it stop for directions? Not without a lot of nagging.

Scientists at the University of Ulm in Germany have found new evidence to explain those frequent disagreements about who's lost, and who isn't. They've found that men and women use different parts of the brain for navigation — and might not define being lost in exactly the same way.

These researchers scanned the brains of 12 men and 12 women as they tried to escape a three-dimensional, virtual reality maze. They found men in the study used a part of the brain called the hippocampus for navigation, while women relied upon the right prefrontal cortex to find their way around.

Men escaped the virtual reality maze in an average of two minutes and 22 seconds, while it took women three minutes and 16 seconds to perform the same task. The study's authors suggest men can find their way out of unfamiliar places better than women. (If we ignore the fact the maze was probably designed by a man).

These scientists speculate enhanced activity in the cortex reflects an effort by women to keep landmarks in mind, while the hippocampus activity in men is needed for the geometric approach. This might also explain a man's reluctance to stop and ask for directions.

We know where we are. We just don't know where anything else is.

Personal experience seems to bear this out. I've found that women can find any place they have been before, while men are much more comfortable with street names and a map.

That's why men have trouble asking directions from a woman. The language is different.

A woman will start naming landmarks. "Do you know where the Big Bear is? You go past McDonalds and turn this way at the statue. It's just down the road a ways from there."

I'm thinking, "Look lady, I barely know what town I'm in! If I knew where that stuff was I wouldn't need directions. How far is 'just down the road,' anyway?"

I'll say, "O.K., I turn to the left and then I'm going south?"

The woman turns toward the wall and starts waving her arm. "O.K., this is south, right? You can go that way if you want, but I'd just turn at the statue if it was me."

It's the same problem when I'm driving and my wife is giving directions. "Turn right here," she says.

I'm thinking, "She means turn to the right, turn precisely here, or this is where you turn?" By the time I figure it out, I've missed the turn.

"It's too late now," she says. "Don't turn here or you'll end up in the mall!"

"That's O.K.," I tell her. "I can get out of a mall. Everybody gets out. That's why there aren't any skeletons in the mall."

Cat Tricks

My long-standing belief that cats won't do tricks is challenged by a story in a Canadian farm paper. The story's author says cats can learn to sit, sit up, shake hands, and wave if given the proper encouragement.

These are good tricks to be sure, but I'm not sure they would work for our kitty. Our cat is more accustomed to "Come in!" "Get out!" "Off the screen!" and "Scram!"

My kitty would be horribly confused by commands like, "Sit," "Shake hands," and, "Wave."

I'm not saying other cat owners shouldn't teach these stunts. I'm just suggesting we consider the past when planning our cat's education.

I've never been a fan of the command, "Sit", for example. Spaniel trainers long ago adopted the word, "Hup" when they want these dogs to sit.

Anyone who misses straight-away pheasants knows there are too many words that rhyme with sit.

The same goes for "sit up." A cat hears this and thinks he's coughed-up another hairball.

Shake hands and wave are good tricks for a kitty, though. These are simple and easy to teach.

Shake hands is taught by touching the cat's paw and commanding, "Shake." The cat should instinctively raise her paw.

Then, the owner grabs the cat's paw and pretends the animal has learned something.

This trick depends upon the cat's previous training and experience, also. The command, "Shake," should only be taught with a dry cat in the beginning.

We can teach our kitty to wave by holding a treat in front of her nose, just out of reach of her front paws. Move the treat back and forth while commanding, "Wave." The cat will reach for the food and appear to be waving.

It's important that we gauge the size of our cat before teaching any of these tricks. A cougar, for example, will respond to the command, "Wave," by biting your hand off and not appear to be waving at all.

I've found the most effective program for training cats is to learn what the animal wants to do and then command it to do so. If the cat grabs a finger with his paw, we should say, "Shake hands."

If he swats at the Christmas tree bulbs we command, "Wave." If the cat is lying in the driveway we say, "Play dead."

If he doesn't get up, we bury him.

Readers should remember treats are given each time the cat obeys a command, considers obeying, or refrains from climbing the curtains. This means a well-educated cat is going to be extremely fat.

The only way to counteract training obesity is to let the cat become ignorant again. Once the kitty is back to normal his training can be resumed.

It Takes All Kinds

I guess I'll never be rich, but that's O.K. I do enough stupid things as it is. Think of the damage I could do if I had a lot of money.

Besides, I don't think money makes a person happy. This spring's camping trip is a good example.

I was camped in a nice, little park that is accessible only by boat. This is a wonderful place during the week but a disaster on weekends.

It was the Friday before Memorial Day, and the circus was fast arriving. There were boats pulling water skiers, jet skis towing rafts, and inner tubes hauling inner tubes. Some of these people had so much equipment they needed a floating train to get it from one place to another.

"City people," I thought. "They can't have any fun unless there's a horde of humanity and lots of noise."

I was packing-up camp and getting out of there, when two old guys arrived with a boat so big they couldn't get it to the dock. They had to anchor eighty yards out and inflate a raft to get to shore.

These fellows had ropes, buoys, and anchors on all four corners of that behemoth. It looked like the Queen Mary setting up in Boston Harbor.

"I wonder how much cash is tied up in that one?" I thought. "Must have been left over from the divorce."

I rounded the point with my boat and coasted toward the dock to pick up some friends. My smallest friend, Miles, was standing on the dock — casting away. (Miles is about seven, and a heck of a fisherman.)

His Grandpa fizzled out in the hot sun and was sitting in the shade on shore. That's where I would have been if I had any sense.

As I approached the dock I could see Miles had something in the bucket we were using for a live well. "I caught a bass! I caught a bass! Wanna see my bass?" he shouted.

Miles tried to pick up the bucket and drag it down the dock, but it was too heavy.

"I'll have to see it when Grandpa gets here," I told him. "I have to hold the boat to the dock right now."

Just then one of the guys from the Queen Mary came stomping down the dock. He looked like he was having about as much fun as a frog at a sea gull convention.

"How ya doin'? You guys catch anything?" Miles asked.

"We don't fish," the old codger grumbled.

I could see this didn't sit straight with the boy. "What the heck are you doing, if you don't fish!?" was the expression on his face.

"Wanna see my bass?" Miles asked. "I caught him right over there."

The old guy peered in the bucket as he walked by. "That's a bass alright," he mumbled.

Miles looked over at me with that big smile he always has. Then he shrugged his shoulders and arms as if to say, "Well, I guess it takes all kinds."

Don't Mess With The Cook

Here we go again. The Associated Press reports the U.S. Department of Agriculture wants to drop restrictions on the amount of soy products that can be served in school meals.

Why would they have restrictions on soy products in school meals? That was left over from a previous administration.

The new proposal would allow schools and day-care centers to serve more tofu, veggie burgers, and other meat substitutes. The reasoning is this would help schools meet dietary guidelines for fat content of school meals.

We've come a long way from the days when the cooks called the shots. Katy Kessler was the cook at my school, and she'd roll over in her grave if she knew what funnels down from Washington these days.

Katy didn't fool around with dietary guidelines. She lived by the old maxim: "It doesn't matter what you serve; it's what they eat that counts."

She knew what we ate, too. We had to walk by the serving counter to empty our trays and utensils, and if you didn't eat something, you'd better have a pretty good story.

Katy's goal was to make sure everyone got a good meal and ate more than they spilled. That meant the food had to be tasty — and it was.

We had sloppy Joes and tomato soup on Mondays, chipped beef with gravy on Tuesdays, and chicken ala king on Wednesdays. Friday was fish day. If the Kuhns family hadn't been Catholic we might never have seen any fish.

Can you imagine a USDA dietitian walking into Katy's kitchen and suggesting she might serve more tofu? "I'll tofu you!" she'd probably say.

Readers may recall the national outrage when Republicans tried to declare ketchup a vegetable back in the '80's. Democrats were so upset, they could barely talk.

Let's face it, a lot of kids eat more ketchup than anything else. We'd better classify it as something if it's going to be half of their diet.

Some folks say the USDA is just trying to save money by substituting soy products for meat. I kind of doubt that. You wouldn't produce that many regulations if you were trying to save money.

School cooks are resourceful, though. These people can look at a bag of beans and see chili. They've learned how to take a small budget, plus a barrel of commodities, and turn it into meals.

Katy's tomato soup was a good example. Her tomato soup was a deep shade of orange and really quite tasty.

When I think about commodities available in those days, I'm almost sure that soup was 80% milk; and the rest was probably ketchup.

Sport Or Revenge

While I strongly doubt this column will ever be printed, I felt I had to write it anyway. (Just kidding. I always wanted to say that.)

I knew they were going to print it. Otherwise I wouldn't bother to write it.

A recent letter to a New York farm paper reminded me of that famous phrase, "I know you aren't going to print this, but..." Of course they are going to print it.

That's what newspapers do: Print stuff.

Newspapers love letters to the editor, and they'll print almost anything. (Within limits, of course.)

I should know. I've been writing this column for nearly 20 years, and papers are still printing it. Some folks have been writing letters to the editor longer than that, and nobody has stopped them, either.

Still it's not unusual to see a letter begin with the thought, "I know this will never be printed, but...;" or the challenge, "I dare you to print this!"

Even more frightening was the conclusion to a letter in a Canadian farm paper. The writer said, "I will not utter a challenge for you to print this letter. If you do, thank you, and please withhold my name and address because I fear a police raid on my premises."

Hey, lighten up! If the police or the mental health officials got names out of the newspaper, I would have been out of business a long time ago.

A person writing to the newspaper has every right to express his or her views, and we as readers have every right to agree or disagree. The letter writer in New York wanted to explain that the New York Dept. of Environmental Conservation is "spending taxpayers' money to breed ringneck pheasants for the less than 4% of New York state residents who hunt." This is being done through the 4-H Pheasant Program.

The writer says these pheasants are a non-native species, originally from China, and accustomed to being fed by humans. "When they are released in the fall, what chance will they have?" she asks.

(A better chance than they had in China would be my guess.)

The writer goes on, "In some areas, upon release, the birds are actually picked up and spun around so that they become disoriented in an effort to make the killing easier for the 'sportsmen'."

I get a kick out of letters like these. They always give me the feeling the writer has been picked up and spun around so that they become disoriented. This country has kids running around killing each other, and some folks would rather worry about dizzy pheasants.

The writer states she raises chickens for their eggs and is not against eating meat. The idea of killing something for sport is what bothers her.

I have never raised pheasants, but I have killed them for sport. I have extensive background with raising chickens, however.

My experience would suggest pheasants are killed for sport, but chickens are almost always killed for revenge.

Sheep On The Green

This year's British Open golf tournament provided an interesting look at the long and storied history of the game. Those who think golf was conceived by a wee Scotsman with a gnarled stick will be happy to learn that is probably correct.

Television viewers were reminded that livestock played a vital role in constructing the first golf courses. Historians surmise grazing sheep created fairways on the old courses of Ireland and Scotland.

Experts say bunkers were formed in places where sheep sought refuge from the storm. Clubhouses were established in places the Scotsmen sought refuge from the sheep — or their wives. Many of these early golfers never left the clubhouse; a tradition carried forward to this day.

Historians speculate that rabbits created the first golf greens by nibbling the most tender grasses on the links. The male rabbit would dig a hole near the center of this short grass and these burrows became the first golf holes.

I've often wished rabbits were still digging golf holes. This would prevent some diabolical greenskeeper from placing the hole four feet from the edge of the green.

No one knows for sure how a flag appeared in the rabbit's burrow on those early courses. Few rabbits had the where-with-all to buy a flag in those days.

Some believe the rabbit would wave his flag when he saw a group of golfers leaving the clubhouse. This might sound silly on the surface, but quite a few denizens of the clubhouse have reported stranger sights than that.

I am not a golf historian, but I have played on courses that seem to have been designed by sheep. I've also played on fairways sporting various amounts of forage.

These fairways weren't actually on the golf course, but close enough to allow a shot or two before folks begin yelling about some idiot playing out of bounds.

The main thing about playing through the pasture is to allow plenty of room for your backswing. Anyone who hits a bull in the teeth with his mashie can expect to be penalized in some way.

The same goes for hitting the ball toward a flock of sheep. Folks who raise sheep will tell us these animals can survive almost anything if they want to.

Sheep are very cult-oriented, though. If one decides it's time to die, a wayward golf ball can kill the entire bunch.

The lie of your ball is critical when the course is maintained by livestock. If the ball appears plugged in a soft spot about the size of a frisbee, don't hit it. Take all of the penalties necessary, but don't hit it!

I read recently that a man on the Oregon coast wants to create a golf course modeled after the ancient courses. The course is supposed to feature grazing sheep.

This might not mean much to the average golfer. But it sounds to me like an excellent place to sell some sheep.

A Farmer's Tan

A recent piece by New York school teacher, farmer, and columnist John Sillick reminds me of our national obsession with suntans. John says when he takes off his shirt to go swimming at family get-togethers his siblings and their broods laugh at him and his "farmer tan."

"My arms are dark, but my torso is very white. It's almost like I have a white tee-shirt on," he says.

John wonders if farmers are the only folks who get a unique type of tan. "Is there a banker's tan or a postal worker's tan?" he asks.

I'm sure there is. The farmer's tan results from the need to exclude dust and chaff. Other occupations must have similar peculiarities.

A banker's tan should be rich and full — like the bank. His face and arms might be tan with a few wrinkles, but his palms should be smooth and white.

Postal workers spend most of their time inside and don't get a lot of tan — unless they are on one of those walking routes. Delivery people are tan up to their knees and just above the elbows due to their short sleeves and Bermuda shorts. Those with a lot of dogs on their route are likely to remain pale throughout the year.

Truck drivers are generally tan on their left arm, but their right is white as can be. The one-armed tan of a truck driver is often confused with a veterinarian's tan, but the two are quite different.

The vets' tan extends all the way to the shoulder and may be on either arm. It all depends upon which sleeve they roll up.

Neither truck drivers nor veterinarians have any tan on their legs. If their legs are brown they've been out in the mud or their horse is shedding.

Mechanics have a unique and rusty tan that begins near their ankles and stops a few inches above that. That's the part that sticks out from under the car.

A mechanic is usually covered with dust and grease, which hides any tan he may have. If you clean up a mechanic you'll often find it's just another farmer whose socks are too short.

School teachers can be tan anywhere, depending upon their hobbies. Teachers who farm have the farmer's tan, and many have a golfer's tan or a fisherman's tan.

The best way to identify a school teacher is to ask if they enjoy having the entire summer off. If their face turns red, white, then back to red again, it's a school teacher's tan.

Newspaper columnists are peculiar when it comes to suntans. We spend most of our time in dark and dusty offices, and tend to avoid sunlight — much like a vampire does.

Too much sun is bad for columnists. It fries the brains, and causes us to write in circles. Maybe we should wear a hat?

Swift Fox

Talk about a can of worms. New guidelines for the Conservation Reserve Program have U.S.D.A. administrators scratching their heads, notepads, and other places — trying to find out what's going on.

Readers will recall the Conservation Reserve Program (CRP) was launched in 1986 as a 10-year program to take low producing and severely erodeable cropland out of production. Side benefits included improved wildlife habitat and a huge increase in business for small town coffee shops.

CRP has been a good program for a lot of people, but the jury is divided on the economic impacts for rural communities. Whether you're for it or against it, most everyone agrees the CRP program was relatively simple the first time around.

But now we've got the 1996 Farm Bill with new emphasis for environmental benefits on CRP ground. The new guidelines include points for protection of endangered species. That's where the fun begins.

News reports from Kansas say as many as 1,000 farmers in that state might lose CRP contracts because their land should not have been credited as habitat for the burrowing beetle and the swift fox. Both are endangered species.

Someone complained the swift fox and burrowing beetle were never documented in that part of Kansas, and the U.S.D.A. was thrown into a tizzy.

The U.S.D.A. administrators should be ashamed of themselves. Nobody should be expected to document a swift fox.

One minute he's there and the next he's gone. They don't call him the swift fox for nothing.

Who cares where the fox was yesterday? He could be halfway across Oklahoma by now.

How can you enhance habitat for a creature like that? Turn out some slow chickens?

The same goes for burrowing beetles, as far as I'm concerned. Nobody wants to crawl around a wheat field looking for an underground beetle.

If those farmers say they've got beetles, that's good enough for me. Just check the box: "Burrowing Beetles".

Now I see U.S.D.A. agencies in Oregon and Washington are hoping to get those states designated as a National Conservation Priority area for endangered salmon. They believe this would increase farmers' chances for CRP contracts.

That's a bad idea, I think. The last thing anybody needs is to get tangled up with an endangered species.

If people want to protect critters with CRP contracts, I'd suggest something less conspicuous than a salmon. The Kansas folks had the right idea.

"Sure we've got swift foxes. Well, no you can't see 'em; but once in awhile you'll hear one go by."

Mucking Out The Barn

It was just one little word, but I could see we were headed for trouble. I wrote, "the mud and manure was about two feet deep." The editor changed that to "the mud and manure muck was about two feet deep."

"Let's leave out the word 'muck'," I said. "I don't think we need it."

"I put that in because mud and manure is two things, and we were using the verb 'was'," she explained. "I added the word `muck' to make it singular. Muck is a good farm word, isn't it?"

"No," I said. "And I don't think we need it."

"But you muck-out the stable, don't you?" she countered.

"I suppose you could muck-out a stable," I said. "But I wouldn't do it."

I was reminded of my wife's friend who used to tell her kids to "dung-out their rooms." In all my years on a farm, and all my years working with farmers and ranchers I've never once heard the word "muck," except to describe an organic soil.

Farmers don't have stables, either. Martha Stewart has stables. When farmers have horses, they keep them in a barn.

Furthermore, mud and manure isn't two things when it's found in a barnyard. Mud and manure becomes one thing in a matter of minutes.

It's called "shud," according to an agricultural engineer from Oregon. Everyone who's been through the barnyard knows what that is.

I wanted to suggest "shud" to the editor, but I knew it wouldn't help. We finally agreed to call it a mud and manure mixture, a mix, or combination. (By this point I didn't care what we called it.)

Finally, we got to the end of my basketball story; the part where my neighbor, Jerry, races past me and goes in for a layup. He slips on the haymow floor and hits the mow door going full-speed. Jerry goes sailing out over the barnlot before his shot goes in.

"I ran to the door and realized Jerry left the arena before the ball went through the basket. Maybe I could disqualify the points because the shooter wasn't present? But how could he know he made it?"

"You missed!" I shouted. [End of story.]

The editor tacked on another paragraph.

"I don't think we need the last paragraph," I told her. "I liked the ending the way it was."

"But we need to refer back to the beginning of the story," she said.

"Refer to the beginning?" I thought. I've been writing these things for 16 years; I didn't know you were supposed to refer to the beginning?

My stories have a beginning and an end, but it's not always the same thing. I'm lucky if it's even the same subject!

I was reminded of the first rule of writing: "When you're done, quit." Don't tack on some type of summary. That's the way I've always done it, and I'm not about to change now.

Wolf School

Here's one for you. The U.S. Fish and Wildlife Service plans to spend $40,000 teaching wolves not to kill livestock.

This experiment involves fitting juvenile wolves with collars that produce a mild electric shock. Then a potential victim (such as a calf) is equipped with a transmitter that delivers a jolt of electricity to said wolf when he gets within "biting distance."

Bird dogs have been trained this way for decades. Imagine a biologist running after his wolf yelling, "Come back here you stupid, *&*%, *&*%$#!"

Biologists believe that wolves learn to hunt from their parents. A shock-educated wolf is supposed to teach her pups to kill wildlife such as elk, deer, and buffalo while avoiding all of those things the adult wolf finds shocking.

It's like teaching our kids how to eat. We say, "Yuck, burritos and cream soda! Those things will make you barf!"

The kids say, "That shows what you know. I eat six of these every day."

The wolf experiment takes place at Ted Turner's Flying D Ranch in southwestern Montana. I presume the wolves will be attacking Ted's buffalo while learning not to kill Herefords, Angus, Brahma crosses, Watusi, Scotch Highlanders, sheep, dogs, goats, cats, horses, chickens, pigs, etc.

I should explain these Montana wolves are an endangered species imported from Canada some years ago. Wolves were considered extinct in the western states before the U.S. Fish and Wildlife Service went to Canada and got some more.

These Canadian wolves were bred and nurtured in captivity, then released into the northern Rockies. They've been having a wonderful time ever since.

I don't see how we can transplant a Canadian wolf into the U.S and then label her pups an endangered species. It's like your cat having kittens in the oven. That doesn't make them biscuits, does it?

The endangered species act is applied differently to wolves than it is to fish, for example. Wild fish can't even be transplanted from one river to another, let alone imported from Canada.

Fish don't have species like wolves do. Fish have subspecies, strains, runs, sub-runs, and groups of consenting adults.

That's how we get the Puget Sound Fall Chinook, Methow River Spring Chinook, and the Upper Smith Creek Gravel Spawning Under The Trees June 23rd Chinook. All of these have to be saved.

Fish born in a hatchery are called "hatchery fish," even if their ancestors were wild. It's like someone asking if our parents were wild.

We'd have to say, "Probably. But that was many years ago."

Descendants of hatchery fish aren't considered wild, even if they were spawned in the wild. Hatchery fish are often clubbed to death to keep them from competing with endangered "wild fish."

That's because fish are managed by the National Marine Fisheries Service (NMFS), whereas wolves are managed by the U.S. Fish and Wildlife Service. If the NMFS managed wolves those shocking experiments wouldn't be necessary.

Those Montana Lupuses would be sent back to Canada and clubbed to death if they tried to return.

Woodchopper

I'm finally ready. I got the stock finished for my shotgun, and now I'm ready to go bird hunting.

This stock isn't that bad, considering. Considering it's the first gunstock I ever made — and considering most of my tools are remnants from the Iron Age.

The stock fits my old double-barreled Fox I bought when I was 16. That old gun and I have been through the swamp a time or two.

You can't buy a gun like mine anymore. Partly because it's a 16-gauge, and partly because nobody wants a gun like mine. I can barely find shells for it.

My old gunstock developed a serious crack a couple of years ago, and I decided I could make my own. A friend gave me a slab off a black walnut tree, and now I have a classic example of the gun-makers' art. Well, "art" might be stretching things a bit.

There were a few setbacks in this stock-making endeavor: Like the day I stuck an 18-inch drill bit in 14 inches of wood; and the time I noticed the gun's action was slightly smaller than the space I had created for it.

But I got the drill bit out, and I used a little "wood enhancer" around the action. The stock turned out pretty good for a wood chopper like me.

My stock is straight (no pistol grip) and has a bit of cast-off like the old English doubles. Cast-off is a lateral bend in the stock away from the gunner, designed to place his or her eye more directly behind the rib between the barrels.

Cast-on is a bend in the opposite direction. Cast-on is not often needed, unless one's eyes bug-out a great deal or the chin has taken a little too much recoil.

American guns generally don't have cast-off or cast-on, partly because American guns generally aren't side-by-sides. One doesn't need such intricacies for an auto-loader or a pump. (I always close my eyes when shooting those things, anyway.)

The old stock-makers gave cast-off to their doubles by soaking the stock in hot oil and bending it. My stock got its bends more naturally.

I simply fitted the stock to the gun; then when I looked at it I exclaimed, "Hot dog! It's got a little cast-off."

My son looked at the stock and said, "How come this side is flatter than that side?"

"That's cast-off," I said. "All the famous stock-makers are doing that now."

Then, I whacked 1/2 inch off the butt of the stock and fitted it back on — to cover the bolt that goes up the center and connects to the mechanism. This results in one of those classic butt-plates everyone has been talking about.

So now I'm ready, and I'm going bird hunting. We'll see if I shoot any better than I did with my old stock.

My son assures me I will. He says I'm extremely unlikely to shoot any worse.

How To Kill A Carrot

I don't think I'll ever be a vegetarian. The only meal I eat that doesn't feature meat is breakfast — and that's mostly eggs.

Even eggs are off limits for strict vegetarians. Eggs come from animals after all, and who knows which one might have become a chicken if I hadn't fried it.

The vegetarian diet centers on philosophy and ethics for a lot of people. There's something about eating animals and raising them for food that some folks find offensive.

People who grew up on a farm generally have no problem with consuming meat. We've seen animals come and go and understand most of these critters wouldn't exist at all if they couldn't be used for food.

That's my philosophy, I guess. If the Good Lord didn't want us to eat animals, he wouldn't have made them out of meat.

We need to respect the beliefs of others, of course. Each of us probably has some ideas that wouldn't stand up to critical examination.

My nephew from Georgia came to visit last summer, and I was afraid the young man would starve to death before we got him back on his customary ration. Craig eats certain kinds of meat, but we knew he's partial to vegetables.

My freezer full of venison wasn't going to fit the program, so the first thing I did was buy him a pizza.

"What kinds of things do you like on your pizza?" I asked. "Your mom said you only eat certain kinds of meat. So you'll have to tell us what you like."

"If I can kill it, I can eat it," he said. "That generally means chicken and below."

"Good heavens!" I thought. "The boy is an animal. He wants to kill his own meat!"

Then I realized my nephew meant he could only eat things he wouldn't feel so bad about killing. Less intelligent animals like chicken, fish, crabs. (Chicken and lower on the evolutionary scale.)

"Oh, I'll bet you could kill a pig," I suggested. "Or a pepperoni. I'm sure you could kill a pepperoni."

"Nope, I couldn't kill a pig; and I can't eat it if I don't know what's in it," he said.

So Craig got a vegetarian pizza, and I'd have to admit it looked a lot better than the pizza I ordered. I'd just like to have that vegetarian job with some pepperoni on top. Then, we'd have some real food.

We had a good visit with Craig, and we didn't make him eat any deer meat.

I've learned over the years that I can kill a deer about as easily as a chicken. After hiking around rockslides, banging my knees on boulders day after day, I get the vindictive notion that somebody is going to have to pay for this.

Overconfident

I'm afraid we have gone too far. In our quest to raise self-esteem in children, we have made incompetence a virtue.

A New York Times News Service story says Professor David Dunning at Cornell University has found self-confidence and incompetence tend to go together. A series of studies by Dunning and graduate student Justin Kruger showed that students who did poorly on various types of tests grossly overestimated their scores, while those who did well had a tendency to underestimate their abilities.

Dunning theorizes the same skills needed for competence are required for recognizing incompetence. Therefore, the most incompetent generally think they are pretty good.

Is everyone with me here? I've always thought my writing was clear, but professor Dunning's study makes me a little nervous.

Personal experience seems to agree with Dunning's research. The professor says college students who do badly on a test will spend hours in his office trying to convince him his answers are wrong.

He says people may tend to overestimate their abilities because feedback is absent in many instances. He mentions other situations, such as golf, where awareness of incompetence is inevitable. "In a golf game, when your ball is heading into the woods, you know you're incompetent," he says. The professor doesn't golf with the same folks I do. When their ball is heading for the woods they say, "Man, I sure hit that one solid." Or, "I tried to hook it, but these clubs are getting worn."

I played a round of golf a few years ago with a fellow who was supremely confident. He would be hitting his eighth shot from a fairway bunker with the utmost confidence his next one would go in. (He beat me by several strokes.)

Dunning's research squares with other studies showing the majority of the population considers themselves above average in all sorts of abilities, even though this is statistically impossible. We might call this the Lake Wobegon syndrome. "Where all the women are strong, all the men are good looking, and all the children are above average," as Garrison Keillor says.

Not everyone agrees with Dunning's conclusions. A psychology professor at the University of California Riverside said he suspects most lay people have only a vague idea of the meaning of "average" in statistical terms. (What does that tell us?)

I don't know who to blame, but education must have something to do with it. If educators are going to take credit for everything, they can take some of the blame.

A recent report, for example, says school children in California did poorly in reading. A school official in that state said that concerns him because this news report might lower the self-esteem of California's students.

Comedian Jay Leno took a crack at that one. "How are they going to find out?" Leno asks. "They surely can't read about it in the newspaper!"

Piano Room

This is my day to clean the piano room. I call it the piano room because there's a piano in there. My wife calls it the sports room, because 80 percent of the contents is sports equipment.

Now, I ask you, "Which is bigger? A piano or a sleeping bag?" I rest my case.

Calling this the piano room relieves me of any responsibility for its condition. Everyone knows I can't play one of those things.

I found some things I had forgotten about, like our old black and white television with the 12-inch screen. That's the best television we ever owned: It only gets two channels.

I see folks switching channels on these newer TV's — with cable access and 88 channels — and wonder, "Why can't we just shoot the thing?"

Our piano-sports room is home to other things, too, like my North Woods snow shoes and Connie's old phonograph records. I'm not sure which is more useful.

I discovered a perfectly preserved coyote tail — and four

bags of shotgun shell casings. These might come in handy someday.

Here's a leash and a pile of dog collars. We've got collars for everything from a Chihuahua to a Great Dane.

I found a bell for a sheep and a set of shears. We sold the sheep years ago, but there might still be one in the piano room for all I know.

I uncovered some backpacks, two belly boats, and a box of clay birds. Here are some old sheets, carpet samples, and upholstery for a boat we used to have.

Some folks would have a yard sale and get rid of this stuff, but I can't do that. One never knows when these things will come in handy.

I've stored books on how to cook over hot rocks and bake chicken in a shell made of mud. One never knows when the electricity will go out.

Any book that hasn't been read in 20 years goes to the barn. I don't know what happens to them after that.

How about these old stereo speakers? They must be too good to put in the barn.

The hardest part for me is finding a place for my fishing rods. I only have a few, of course, but the one-piece rods are too long to sit in a corner.

An old gun rack solves that problem. I just hang the rack on the wall and fill it with rods.

I used to worry about making holes in the walls to hang things up, but not anymore. Now I'm just happy if I can see the walls.

The room is clean now, though. A person can walk in without stepping on much of anything.

We can find almost everything, too. Except maybe the piano.

Consumer Confidence

I guess I'll never understand economics. The experts say our economy is going gangbusters, consumer confidence has reached an all-time high, but personal savings have reached an all time low.

This seems backwards to me. It seems folks with a lot of confidence would be saving for the future — instead of spending every nickel they can get ahold of.

Today's consumers remind me of an old fellow a friend was telling me about. This old guy is getting up in years and likes to joke about his age.

"I'm getting so old," he said, "I won't even buy green bananas, anymore."

Or another old codger a different friend described to me. This man lived way out in the boonies and didn't have a car, so he only got into town every month or so.

My friend saw the old-timer on the street one winter day and asked how he was doing. "Oh, I'm fine," he said. "I've got some venison in the shed, and a little bit of firewood cut up.

"I don't cut much wood at one time," he explained. "I

could die most any day, you know."

Modern day consumers seem to take the opposite view. The more confident they get the less wood they cut.

I blame the whole thing on credit cards. Credit cards have made spending much too easy.

Just before Christmas my wife and I received several blank checks from credit card companies. Letters accompanying the checks suggested, "There must be lots of things you would like to buy — but probably can't afford. These checks will help you buy it, anyway."

"Don't worry about repaying anything. We'll tell you about that later."

These companies must have thought we ran out of checks and didn't know where to get more? Maybe they were hoping we were so stupid as to think this was free money, and we wouldn't have to pay it back?

Earlier this fall I got a call from a company that helps people consolidate their debts. "Hello, Mr. Pond? This is Martha from `such and such' company and I'm calling to tell you about our new program for consolidating your bills and reducing your debt."

I thought for a few seconds and said, "We don't have any debt."

The caller stammered a little and said, "But you own your home don't you?"

"That's right," I said.

"Maybe we can help you reduce your mortgage payment," she suggested.

"We paid off our mortgage," I told her and hung up the phone.

People like me are a tele-marketer's worst nightmare. When you make calls at random, you never know when you'll get a complete nut.

A Good Salesman

Most of us have a negative image of salespeople — except for the ones we know personally. Then we like them just fine.

A couple of years ago I read a column by a man who gives sales seminars. At one session this fellow asked his audience, "How many of you didn't like salespeople before you got into sales?"

Nearly everyone raised their hands. Then he asked, "Now that you are a salesperson yourself, how many of you still don't like salespeople?

Almost everyone raised their hands again. This fellow says this just proves salespeople should do their best not to act like salespeople.

A good example of this was a car dealer who tried to sell my wife and me an old junker soon after we were married. An old junker was all we could afford, so that wasn't a problem; but this guy rubbed me the wrong way from the beginning.

It wasn't just his brown and white saddle shoes or his

funny, little hat with the chicken feather in it. This salesman wanted to sell us a car and get us off the lot before the whole thing exploded.

We looked at a couple of vehicles and told the salesman we'd have to think about it. That's when he said, "These prices are only good for tonight. If you come back in the morning, it will cost you more."

This man has become one of the biggest car dealers in the country, but I still wouldn't buy so much as a floor mat from him.

Some of the best salesmen I've known are retired farmers. Farmers have been selling things to each other for so long they know exactly what to say and when to say it.

My dad quit farming at the ripe old age of 44 and began selling appliances for a friend who owned an appliance shop. Like any good salesperson, Dad understood that some folks have a hard time buying things.

They know they need it, but they just can't decide on the model, or the color, or the payment plan. It's up to the salesperson to help them make up their minds.

That's what happened to a guy who walked into the Appliance Shop one day, looking for a television. Dad showed him all of the models and described the features for him but the fellow couldn't make up his mind.

He wasn't real sure he needed a TV in the first place, and all of the choices seemed overwhelming.

Finally, Dad said, "If you want to go home and think about the TV, that's probably a good idea; but you might as well buy an antennae while you're here. That way you'll be all set up when you get the TV."

The fellow bought his antennae and left as happy as could be. This made Dad famous down at the coffee shop.

"Who else," they asked, "could sell an antennae to a man who didn't even have a television?"

Rooting For The Team

College football fans have been on an emotional roller coaster the past few weeks. It doesn't matter if you're rooting for Nebraska or Slippery Rock, the feeling is the same. Except Slippery Rock's roller coaster costs a lot less.

November 22 was rivalry weekend. Michigan beat Ohio State, Tennessee beat Kentucky, and Washington State is still trying to find out if the Rose Bowl is played in California like it was in 1931.

I watched the Ohio State-Michigan game. Like other Ohio State alums, I was crushed.

Football fans will recall Michigan beat Ohio State eight times and tied once in the ten years John Cooper coached the Buckeyes.

Some folks blame the coach, but I don't. I've watched the Buckeyes for years, and as far as I can tell the coach doesn't even play.

Like other football experts I was yelling, "Come on Cooper, open up the offense!" Ohio State threw two interceptions, and I moaned, "Whatever happened to Woody Hayes?"

I was reminded of the night my high school buddy, Ron, and I sat in the stands at a football game. Ron was a bit of a cut-up in those days, and our teachers claimed the two of us together were like a match and a gas leak.

The game was nearing the end of the first half, and our team was way behind. Ron and I had been shouting encouragement all night.

"Hold on to the ball, butterfingers! What's the matter with you guys? Why don't you put in the cheerleaders?"

We thought it was encouragement, anyway.

That's when I noticed a woman sitting in front of us. She was all dressed up with her hair pulled back in one of those tight, little buns popular in the early 60's. I thought this woman looked familiar but put it out of my mind.

Just then our center snapped the ball. The quarterback handed-off to the halfback, who tossed the ball back to the quarterback, who gave it to the fullback, who dropped it on the ground — and the other team recovered the fumble.

"What's the matter with you guys? Where are they getting those plays?" Ron shouted.

That's when the lady with the hornet's nest hairdo turned around — and I remembered where I had seen her. She was the coach's wife!

This woman looked at my buddy in such a way I worried she might melt the bolts in the bleachers we were sitting on. Even after all these years, I have no idea how a woman could stare at someone so long without blinking. (Unless the tension on that coiffure had something to do with it.)

That football game was a real lesson for me. To this day, I never sit down at a sporting event without asking, "Is this seat taken? And is there anyone around here who is a good friend of the coach?"

1/2 West Virginian

The U.S. Constitution has taken a beating recently. Actually the Constitution has been getting pummeled for a long time, but the process seems to be heating up.

A Census Bureau plan to use a "sampling method" in the 2000 census shows how far we've veered from the Constitution. That historic document requires a census every 10 years based upon actual enumeration, but census officials are having trouble defining "enumeration." They apparently believe it means, "A reasonable estimation, according to our best judgment, and what we think would be good for the country."

Democrats say sampling would help correct the undercounting of minorities that occurred in the previous census. Republicans are saying, "No way, Harold. A person is a person, and if you can't count 'em, they don't count."

"Besides," Republicans say, "sampling would be open to manipulation by unscrupulous persons." They didn't mention any names but the innuendo is pretty clear, I think.

I can't speak for others, but I don't want to be sampled. I want to be counted — just like the authors of our Constitution intended.

If I'm estimated through some sampling process, I might be characterized as 1/2 or 3/4, something less than a whole person. Or, I could be more than one person, like the little girl in my sister-in-law's 5th grade class.

My sister-in-law, Barb, teaches fifth grade in Newark, Ohio, where the population is a divergent mix of iron workers' sons, coal miner's daughters, and Longaberger basket-makers. Many of Barb's students are descended from the Eastern Europeans who came to Ohio to work in the mines near the turn of the century. Others are Irish, German, or more recent arrivals we call minorities — no matter how many there are.

Barb thought it would be fun for her students to learn more about their family's heritage. This information could add interest to lessons in world history and social studies, and should do no harm as long as it doesn't spill over into recess.

So my sister-in-law designed a "roots project" encouraging her students to ask their parents about their family's heritage. Where did their great-grandparents come from? Their great-great-grandparents? Were they Russian, English, Hispanic, African-American, German?

How did they get to this country? Boat, train, plane? Duh? (Well, most of the questions were good.)

Soon kids were returning with their data. Some were full of information. Others barely knew who their parents were, let alone their great-grandparents.

Most memorable was a little red-haired girl in the front row. She said, "My momma said to tell you I'm half German, half Irish, and half West Virginian."

That puts this whole census issue in perspective, as far as I'm concerned. Sampling may work when it comes to minorities, but you have to be sharp when you count West Virginians.

Roadkill

The Governor of New York and the state legislature have taken some ribbing about that state's new "cat law." Governor Pataki recently signed legislation requiring motorists in New York to make "reasonable effort" to find the owner, or report to police when a cat is killed on the highway.

News reports say the new law simply adds cats to existing statutes requiring motorists to search for owners of dogs, cows, and horses that fall prey to autos. I would hope sheep, goats, hampsters, and guinea pigs are accorded similar consideration.

There's nothing wrong with the intentions of this law, but I have to question the wisdom of legislating courtesy and common sense. Responsible motorists will make reasonable efforts to find the animal's owner, anyway. And irresponsible drivers will jump out of their car yelling, "Whose cat is this?" and be on their way.

The crux of New York's cat law is the concept of "reasonable effort." What constitutes reasonable effort? That's not an easy question.

First a driver must determine if a cat has actually been killed. Not a simple task (as I will explain later). Cats didn't get their "nine lives" reputation by being a bunch of cream puffs.

Then, the motorist must describe the dead animal to nearby residents. No piece of cake, either.

A homeowner asks, "What does the cat look like?"

The driver says, "Well it's about a foot-and-a-half long and half-an-inch thick."

"No," she says, "I mean what did it look like before you hit it?"

"Scared!" the driver replies.

Dogs are even worse. We could ask a friend of my secretary about that.

This young lady was driving to church one evening when a dog ran out in front of her car, and she hit it. She got out of the car and could readily see the creature was just a mass of blood and fur.

The young woman thought the poor thing might still be alive, so she lifted the hatch-back on her car and lifted it in. No easy feat when you are dressed up for an evening church service.

Then, our conscientious young woman started looking for the dog's owner. She drove up and down the road, knocking on doors and describing the animal to everyone she could find. No one owned a dog that looked anything like this one.

Finally, she decided the creature wasn't going to last much longer. She would take it to the all-night veterinarian across town. Maybe he could save it.

The young lady arrived at the vet's office 20 minutes later. The vet walked out to her car while she waited for the sad news about her canine companion. The vet returned quickly.

"I have some bad news for you Ma'am," he said.

"Your dog is doing fine, but your dog is not a dog. It's a coyote! And you aren't going to like what he's doing to your car!"

Save A Tree

I'm always a little behind with my column topics. I can keep up in January and February when nobody cares what's happening, but I get behind in the spring and fall.

Maybe I should slow down for a few months and try to get back in sync? That's what happened to a farmer I used to know.

One year my farmer friend got so far behind he wound up harvesting his corn in May. "It's all in how you look at it," he said. "Some folks might think I'm seven months behind, but I prefer to see it as five months ahead."

That's why anyone who reads this column after Christmas should consider it a good start for next year. (Only 360 shopping days to go.)

Folks who need a last minute Christmas gift might consider the idea cooked-up by two Oregon entrepreneurs. According to a story in the Portland *Oregonian* these two fellows have decided the ideal gift for most occasions is a tree.

Not a dead tree to put up and decorate, or a live tree to plant in the yard, but a real tree — to be left in the woods and enjoyed by future generations of bears, chipmunks, and presumably woodpeckers.

These men have formed a company called "Save A Tree" that permits a person to buy a 10-foot-tall tree for $50, a 24-footer for $100, or a 48-footer for $200. These trees then go into a trust and will never be logged, the partners say.

The tree buyer gets an identifying plaque, certificate of ownership, and a map showing where his or her tree is located. All of these trees are supposedly growing in the Blue Mountains of Eastern Oregon.

This is a nice idea for folks who want to get involved in forest management, I think. A plan such as this might eliminate much of the animosity that has accrued between timber owners and logging protesters in recent years.

Just last week I saw a news clip about a girl named "Butterfly" who has been sitting in a redwood tree in California for nearly a year to protest a timber sale. If these redwoods were owned by a company like Save A Tree we could buy that girl her tree, and she could come down and take a bath.

There might be a downside to the Save A Tree philosophy, though. I call it the "Sad Christmas Story."

This story takes place in the National Forest one December when families begin arriving to cut a Christmas tree. It's about one little fir standing tall and straight, hoping someone will take him home to celebrate the holidays with their family.

But try as he might, the little fir just couldn't compete with the fancy pines or the elegant spruce that grew close by. One by one the families came to the forest to cut their Christmas trees, but nobody noticed the little fir who wanted so badly to celebrate the holidays with a family.

Finally, the day before Christmas, the little fir tree had almost given up hope — when suddenly, he heard a rustling in the brush! "Was it someone coming to take him home for Christmas?!"

Nope, it was a big flock of woodpeckers, and they wiped him out.

Fair Judges

Nothing beats a county fair for unbridled excitement. One of the moms explained it this way, "If I had one more kid or one more entry, I'd be totally out of my mind!"

Insanity isn't a prerequisite for exhibiting at the fair, but it certainly doesn't hurt anything. Fairs are for kids, and folks who can think like a kid are sure to have the most fun.

The main thing about county fairs is not to take them too seriously. We shouldn't take it personally if our pumpkin gets a white ribbon, for example. Nor should we suggest the judge doesn't know a pumpkin from a cucumber.

Folks forget how much pressure judges are under when they attend small county fairs. Judges are often the only strangers on the grounds, and that has to take a toll on a person.

Being an outsider, plus the desire to present a neat appearance, makes a judge feel like a well-dressed chicken thief. It's not easy judging a show where everyone in the audience knows the Champion gelding is still the most worthless nag in the whole county.

Exhibitors aren't totally harmless, either. A judge can

destroy an exhibitor's confidence with a white ribbon, but the exhibitor can destroy a judge's boot by encouraging his goat to wet on it.

Still, the judge has the upper hand and deserves a certain amount of respect. Most judges command respect by dressing and looking the part.

Beef cattle judges, for example, are easily recognized by their big hats and shiny belt buckles. Beef judges walk real slow and avoid quick movements. The last time a beef judge made a sudden move, a big, red steer took out the cotton candy concession.

Poultry judges are distinguished by their white smocks and flighty manner. Poultry judges are always early and seem afraid the chickens will get away before the show begins.

Swine judges generally wear a Moorman's Feed cap and some old shoes or rubber boots. Hog judges are easy to get along with. They have the ability to call a pig a pig in such a way that everyone thinks they've paid the animal a compliment.

In contrast to beef and swine judges, sheep judges have no special attire. They used to have a hat, but the dog ate it.

The most difficult thing for any judge is when they're asked to evaluate something outside their specialty. This happens when the show management forgot to get a rabbit judge — or a herd of guinea pigs shows up unexpectedly.

Instances such as these cause show management to make some assumptions. They say things like, "Guinea pigs? Sounds like the swine judge to me," or, "Rabbits have floppy ears, don't they? Let's ask the sheep judge."

Experienced judges have no trouble with these situations. They simply say, "These are the cutest guinea pigs I've ever seen. We'll just give them all blue ribbons."

Making Hay

Farming has changed so much many of us who grew up in the country would barely recognize what farmers do today. Of all the technological advances new forage handling systems are the most intriguing for me.

A news release from Vermeer Manufacturing describes the new Vermeer Ensiler — designed to simplify the process of baling and wrapping high moisture hay (called balage). The new process is said to eliminate extra hours, extra equipment costs and extra trips over the field by actually wrapping the bale with plastic film before it hits the ground.

"After the bale is formed, a hydraulically-powered bale cradle extends to the back and turns the bale as it's being wrapped. An automatic swing-arm assembly revolves around the bale, stretching the film tightly to provide an airtight seal. Pretensioner arms stretch the plastic film 55% to maximize film usage."

Then, someone comes along with Vermeer's BH1000 Bale Handler (introduced earlier this year) and "gently lifts and transports the bale to its final storage site." These high moisture bales weigh up to 2,000 lb.

The system is operated completely from the tractor seat, using a single hydraulic lever. Whatever happened to the dusty, old balers and sweaty haymows of our youth?

Maybe I'm old-fashioned, but I look at machinery like this and wonder, "How much does it cost?" And, "What if something breaks?"

We surely can't fix it. We won't have any baling wire!

That's not the way we made hay when I was a kid. I grew up in the East — where it used to rain in the summer. We cured hay as fast as we could, baled it, and ran for the barn with it.

Our hay never had a "final storage site." Sometimes it was in the right barn, and sometimes it wasn't. If we needed the hay somewhere else, we just had to drag it.

My brother and I tried stacking bales outside and covering them one year. This proved to be an excellent way to consolidate our forage — making it much easier to pick up after it rotted.

Haymaking was far from a one-man operation in those days. We needed a kid to cut the hay, one to rake it, another to drive the tractor on the baler, and a guy to stack bales on the wagon.

Then, we had a kid bringing empty wagons to the field and a man with a lot of nerve catching the hay forks that lifted bales into the mow. A relatively small boy or girl pulled the trip rope, dropping hay into the mow and pulling the forks back out.

There were seven kids in my family, so we could pretty much do everything ourselves.

Sometimes I marvel at the things a farmer is forced to do today. I see the expensive machinery and all of the stresses it causes.

At times like these I think, "I know birth control has done a lot of good, and it's probably been great for women. On the other hand, it's just about ruined farming."

Primitive Science

I don't think I'll ever understand biology. I spent years studying wildlife management, but I'm not sure I learned anything.

Just last week I was fishing with a friend who knows more about the birds and the bees than I'll ever master. The fish weren't biting, so we amused ourselves watching groups of water birds paddling near shore.

Suddenly one of the birds emitted a high-pitched whistle. "Do you know what's making that sound?" my friend asked.

"It's that bird over there," I said.

"No, I mean do you know what kind of bird that is? It's a Western grebe," he instructed. "Those are the ones you see skittering across the water in the TV commercials."

"I always wondered what those were," I admitted. "I thought they might be grebes of some sort."

I tend to blame my biological innocence on my background in agriculture. While others see a big flock of geese and marvel at their grace and beauty, I look at these birds and calculate how much wheat they're eating.

When biologists are doing their best to mimic Mother Nature, I'm wondering why they can't do things a little more efficiently.

Habitat improvement for salmon is a good example. Fish biologists have adopted a practice of collecting spawned-out hatchery salmon and scattering them along streams for nutrient enhancement.

Biologists say this imitates the natural cycle of fish spawning and dying, providing nutrients for stream life and future generations of salmon. They call this "science."

I call it primitive. What if farmers operated this way?

What if sheep producers saved up all of their dead sheep and scattered them around the farm for fertilizer? How scientific is that?

Do fish get diseases? Sheep surely do.

I've never tried scattering fish, but spreading sheep is a real headache; I can tell you that. There's just no way to get an even application.

You've got a sheep here, another one over there, and two over here. That's why we invented fertilizer.

What if a fish scatterer throws a salmon toward the stream, and it hits a tree? That fish may never fertilize the stream as intended. (Do they go pick it up and throw it again?)

What if your fish hits another scientist? A really big scientist! That might lead to all sorts of fertilizer.

How many fish can a person carry? How far into the woods do they get?

Why not convert those fish to something a little more manageable — and a little more sanitary. Make a stream fertilizer.

Apply it by air. Put it where you want it. That's science.

Then when someone asks, "Do you know what's causing that smell?" We won't have to say, "I think it's that rotten fish over there."

A Fine Kettle Of Fish

I grew up at a time when folks thought there were only two ways to do things: The "right way" and the "wrong way." People lived by the axiom, "If you don't have time to do it right, how will you ever find time to do it over?"

Those are good principles, I guess, but extremely hard to live by. My experience suggests there are at least three ways to do things, and if you don't have time to do it over, you should never have tried it in the first place.

I generally do things the right way, the wrong way, or my own way. And I seldom do anything right the first time. I try to allot some time to try it again.

My recent fish canning experience is a good example. I smoked some fish a few years ago, but I had never canned fish.

My wife canned lots of stuff before she learned her rights and got a full time job. Now, Connie won't go anywhere near a pressure cooker.

She told me where she hid the canner, though. So I built a smoker, got a new recipe, and went to work with some equipment I had never seen before. In other words, I did it my way.

I had some salmon and some sturgeon and started thawing the fish on Thursday night. I worked for the extension service years ago and knew fish is supposed to be thawed in the refrigerator, rather than on the kitchen counter.

I also know extension home economists will scare you to death if you ask them about food safety. They are right, of course, but scary just the same.

Our fridge was full, so I put the fish outside in a cooler. It was 36 degrees outside, just like the refrigerator. By Saturday night my fish was thawed.

I mixed up the brine: Water, apple juice, soy sauce, salt, brown sugar, onion powder, and garlic powder. (Put it in a crock, keep it cold, and don't go out in public for a few days.)

Sunday morning I was ready to go. Wood, smoker, fish, matches, directions from the extension service.

I read the directions and followed them to the letter as much as possible. Finally, I thought, "If smoking fish was that dangerous, Lewis and Clark wouldn't have found anybody on the West Coast."

I did my best, though. Monday I was ready to can. The fish was kept cold after smoking, like it's supposed to be.

Then, I started looking for jars and lids. Found some of each and filled the jars with fish. Then I went back to find lids the same size as the jars.

Finally, Monday afternoon the fish was canned! I had preserved seven pints of fish in a little more than a weekend.

How did it turn out? I don't know. I'm afraid to open the jars.

You're Not Supposed To Drink It!

The World Trade Organization meetings in Seattle this fall should be a lesson to everyone: Don't go to Seattle when there's a convention going on.

Everyone had their say at the WTO Conference, except maybe the folks who were supposed to participate. Demonstrators were protesting a number of things: Jobs being shipped overseas, environmental degradation, family farms destroyed by global markets, just to name a few.

Even the police got in their licks. They objected to demonstrators in general and protesters in particular.

Many of the anti-WTO demonstrators came from a diverse coalition of groups and individuals. Environmental activists stood beside family farmers. Church leaders locked arms with longshoremen and union advocates.

I suspect we could engage all of these groups in one huge conversation, and they would kill each other before it was over.

I tend to agree with folks who worry about our growing dependence on world trade. I realize, however, there are smarter people than I who would disagree with me completely.

That's why I'll never be an activist, I guess. I can never

shake the feeling that I could be wrong (or sadly mistaken).

What if I painted a sign, dressed-up like a butterfly, and got blasted with rubber bullets — only to find out I was at the wrong demonstration!? Would that be embarrassing or what?

A few of the folks protesting in Seattle (the anarchists) object to nearly everything. I ran into a fellow like that several years ago.

This man was opposed to a timber company plan to spray spruce budworms with insecticide. He called me and asked if he could come over and talk about the problem.

"Why would he call me?" I thought. I'm very much in favor of pesticides and totally against budworms. That's like calling a fox and asking him to come over and watch some chickens.

I wanted to be fair, though. Remember what I said, "I could be wrong."

So I invited this fellow over with the honest intention of listening to his side. He brought some information that was written by a doctor who knows less about pesticides than I know about world trade.

I listened, though. I really did.

Then I said, "The insecticide the timber company wants to use has a very low toxicity for humans and animals. It's one of the ingredients used in flea powders."

I hunted down my insect control book from the university and showed him the toxicity data. "I don't believe that," he said. "That's from the government."

I later attended a public meeting where state entomologists presented information about the proposed insecticide (active ingredient carbaryl) and the organic alternative, Bacillus Thuringiensis.

The meeting went fine for awhile. Then my acquaintance became quite agitated. Finally he shouted at one of the speakers, "O.K., you can drink Carbaryl, and I'll drink Bacillus Thuringiensis!"

The state entomologist winced at that. "I think I'll just drink bourbon," he said.

Cat Trainer

I guess I'll never be a cat person. There's something about felines that gets under my skin and the cats know it.

Our current kitty is the closest thing to an exception I've seen. That's because I trained her myself.

I know folks say you can't train a cat, but that's because cats are sneaky. They pretend to be stupid so their owners won't try to teach them anything.

Our kitty has learned two tricks I would recommend to all cat owners. She goes outside when I say "out," and she won't come in until I say "in."

This prevents the cat from running through the doorway every time someone opens the door — and from hiding under the couch until I forget about her. The kitty learned these things from constant repetition.

I'm not saying this is an especially smart cat. (I can still beat her at checkers.) I'm just saying cats can be trained once they understand who's boss.

Now that my reputation as a cat trainer is established, I often field questions from others who believe their cat is surely smarter than he acts. The following are some examples:

Dear Mr. Pond:

My cat stays outside most of the time but has a habit of climbing the screen door when he wants in. I've replaced the screen three times. Is there any way to stop this habit?

Signed,
Sick and Tired

Dear Sick:

Your cat needs a refresher in obedience. I would begin by showing him a tennis racquet and asking him to imagine how many cats it would take to make one of these. A banjo will work if you don't have a racquet.

If the cat persists in climbing the door, I would keep the screen and replace the cat.

Dear Mr. Pond:

My friend who lives on a farm wants to give me a kitten. I want a cat that can stay in the house, but my friend says his are "barn cats." What's the difference between a house cat and a barn cat?

Signed,
Puzzled in Pocatello

Dear Puzzled:

About fifty yards.

Dear Mr. Pond:

My cat likes to play outside, but I'm afraid she will go into the neighbor's yard. I've been told cats can pick up toxic substances and then ingest these by licking their feet. Is this true?

Signed,
Fearful in Farmingham

Dear Fearful:

Cats certainly might ingest toxic substances by licking their feet, but this wouldn't be a major concern in my opinion. I've owned a number of cats and have noticed they don't lick their feet as much as one might think.

I think the cats I've owned could walk through toxic substances without much worry. If they sat in those materials, on the other hand, it would kill them for sure.

Get Some Suspenders

Keeping in style has always been a problem for me. The only way I can keep up with fashions is to wear cowboy clothes all of the time. Those never go out of style.

My biggest problem is finding jeans that fit. There are several reasons for this, but the clothing manufacturers certainly deserve part of the blame.

My waist size hasn't changed much. It just moved down a few inches. Why can't clothing manufacturers compensate for things like that?

I could try suspenders, but I grew up in the days when suspenders were for sissies — and bib overalls were considered "barn clothes." Nobody would have been caught dead in a pair of suspenders when I was a kid.

All that has changed. The biggest thing going with kids today is baggy pants and suspenders. These kids had better wear suspenders, because there's no way to hold those pants up if they don't.

My daughter tells me she has seen two kids lose their drawers in the past few months. One was talking on the phone in front of the grocery, and the other was trying to get on his bicycle.

Nobody wore baggy pants when I was a kid. Our jeans were called overalls, and we made sure they were tight in the hips and pegged at the cuff. Anyone who could put his pants on without lying on the floor didn't have enough taper.

Our jeans weren't full of wrinkles, either. That's because my mother had a mangle iron.

A few readers may remember the old mangle irons. Mother called hers the "automatic iron," but there was nothing automatic about it.

This iron had a big, round drum that rotated against a concave to press the clothes. Mother sat in front of it, feeding pants into the machine, much like one would feed a wringer-washer.

The drum was operated by a foot pedal. Each time the concave was pressed against the clothes, a big cloud of steam would belch toward the ceiling. Talk about power; using a mangle iron for wash day was like taking a road-roller to a cookie bake.

There were five boys in our family, and Mother was dedicated to keeping all of our clothes clean. Wash day often looked like an explosion at a Levi's factory.

The automatic iron would press any type of clothes, but Mother only used it for overalls. If you put a tan shirt through this iron, it came out looking like a brown grocery bag.

Jeans rolled from the automatic iron like paper from a typewriter. These pants were brittle. You had to bend them over a chair or slam them in a door a few times to loosen them up so you could crawl in.

Styles change, I guess. Clean, well-pressed clothes were a lot more important in those days than they are now.

I'll tell you one thing, though. Those loose, cotton pants kids are wearing these days wouldn't have lasted two weeks at our house. Mother's automatic iron would have eaten them alive.

Fooling With The Tax Man

This is my day to visit our accountant. I've resolved not to ask any stupid questions this time.

I still can't understand why my dog isn't considered a dependent. Nobody else is claiming him. I can't see why I shouldn't.

That's why I have an accountant, I suppose. My records are pretty good, but I get confused once in awhile.

My biggest mistake this year was underpaying federal unemployment tax. A glitch in my computer worksheet caused me to under-report wages by about $200.

This led to an underpayment of federal unemployment in the amount of $1.94. When I found the error, I promptly sent the IRS a check for $1.94.

I wonder what it costs the government to process a check for $1.94? They probably thought I was fooling with them.

The whole thing reminded me of a story a friend told me about an old codger he used to know.

This fellow (we'll call him Willard) bought a little plot of land at the edge of the desert and proceeded to make himself a home. The property had no buildings when Willard bought it, and the tax assessment was only 18 cents.

Over the years Willard built himself a house out of some wood he found lying around. Then, he built a shop and began piling-up scrap iron, just in case he might ever find a use for it.

I should explain, those were the days when a man might build his own house without building permits — and get away with it. If the house fell on him, everyone just chalked it up to education.

So the county assessor might not have known Willard had some improvements on his property. Or if the assessor knew, he may not have cared.

The neighbors said it would take a pretty good stretch to call Willard's buildings improvements, anyway; so 18 cents was probably about right.

Either way, the taxes never went up or down. Each spring Willard would get a bill for property taxes in the outrageous amount of 18 cents.

The old rascal would pay his taxes right on time, but he never sent them 18 cents. He would always send a quarter, so the assessor's office had to buy a 12-cent stamp to refund his overpayment of seven cents.

That way the county received 18 cents, but it cost them 12 cents to collect it. So they actually only got 6 cents out of the deal! Pretty good, huh?

It was all part of the Sagebrush Rebellion from Willard's point of view. He never could understand what the county was doing with all that money, anyway.

I thought about Willard when I wrote that check for $1.94 and sent it to the IRS. I can't say that transaction made me feel any better, but I'll bet it didn't exactly make their day, either.

Pepper Spray

Here's some good news for bears. A wire service report says the subcommittee on grizzly bear management at Yellowstone National Park has released a draft position paper favoring pepper spray to discourage bear attacks.

The position paper states, "The use of pepper spray as a bear deterrent will reduce the number of grizzly bears killed in self-defense and help promote the recovery and survival of the grizzly bear in the Yellowstone ecosystem."

The subcommittee should be commended for their strong posture on pepper spray. This is far superior to the flat-on-their-back position campers and hikers often assume when squirting bears with repellents.

There is some controversy over the use of pepper spray on bears. The National Park Service prefers spray over firearms, but the bears are griping about the type of pepper folks have been using. They'd like a little salt and some garlic mixed-in.

I know hikers and campers may complain about trying to operate a pressurized can while being chewed by a bear, but that's the price we pay for a healthy ecosystem. Just make sure the bear doesn't eat the can. That would make him sick.

Bear specialists aren't just leaving folks out to dry on this one. They voted to donate $25,000 to the Center for Wildlife Information in Missoula to help produce videos and brochures on the proper use of pepper spray by hunters, outfitters, and recreationists.

The bears wanted recipes, too, but biologists wouldn't spring for that. A bear needs to learn, if he's going to chew on people, he's going to have some sore eyes in the morning.

The wire service report says most of the $25,000 for pepper spray education will be provided by the Forest Service, National Park Service, and state wildlife departments. Where do they get all that money? They must have some bake sales or something.

There's private money here, too. The folks who make the pepper spray are donating $1,000, and the people doing the brochures are giving $5,000. (Give me $25,000 and I'll chip in $5,000, too.)

I'm hoping that outfit in Missoula will ask me to help with their brochures. My limited experience with grizzlies should prove valuable for instructing novices.

I've learned the main thing campers and hikers should remember when going into bear country is to always go in groups. The more the better. A bear can only eat so much.

Second, make sure your pepper spray is readily accessible. If a bear approaches, show him the can. That way he'll know this isn't just another shot of Right Guard he's getting.

Never look directly at a bear. Bears consider this aggressive behavior. Pepper spray works best with your eyes closed, anyway.

The slowest member of a group should try to shoot some spray over his or her shoulder each time the bear gets close. Faster campers should give their spray to slow campers. Slow campers should give their spray to park officials and let them fight the bears.

Otherwise, have a good time in our National Parks and Forests. I'll let you know when the brochures are finished.

Let The Women Do It

Solving the farm problem is always a favorite topic for politicians. Sometimes it's hard to tell which problem these folks are trying to solve but there's always plenty to talk about.

I always thought farm programs are like worming sheep. You may not have the problem, but if you are part of the flock you're going to get the solution.

To understand today's farm policy I think we need to look back about 40 years — when most of these programs were conceived. Those were the days of the family farm.

Nearly all of our farms were small in the 1950's and farm families often had six or seven kids. Labor was plentiful, but those farms weren't very efficient.

Economists of the day recognized U.S. farms had to get bigger and families had to get smaller if we planned to feed the world, and farmers were to enjoy the same standard of living as city people. Many of us can remember economists saying, "The main problem farmers have is there are just too many of them."

Much of the philosophy for today's farm policy was formulated during that period. In those days, the primary impetus for government assistance to farmers was to reduce the number of farms and prevent folks from having kids.

Today's farm programs fit that mold. They are designed to make people quit farming or keep them up all night doing paper work.

The whole thing seems needless to me. If commodity prices and the confusion of farm programs haven't caused a person to give up, I don't know what more the government can do.

They're still working on it though. I got my newsletter today from the local Farm Services Agency (FSA) explaining election procedures for the County FSA Committee.

The newsletter says nominations are now being accepted for a committee member from Local Administrative Area (LAA) #1. I don't know who came up with a moniker like "Local Administrative Area #1", but I can guarantee it wasn't anybody within 1,000 miles of that neighborhood.

The newsletter explains each open position must have at least four nominations and one of these candidates must be a woman, "Although it is certainly encouraged to have more than just one woman nominee."

Now we have quotas for women on county committees?! Who are they trying to kid? Everybody knows farmers wouldn't be serving on these committees if they thought they could get their wives to do it.

I know some women aren't wives and many women are farmers and all that, but I remember the days when organizations had women's auxiliaries.

I've seen this happen more than once. Somebody comes up with a bright idea and then looks around the room for volunteers.

After a long silence, a guy in the back finally says, "Maybe this is something the women would like to do?"

SAD

Here we are again. Time for the annual report on seasonal affective disorder (SAD).

I presume everyone knows that seasonal affective disorder is caused by shorter days, longer nights, and an overabundance of the hormone melatonin. For years I didn't know what caused it, but I was sure I probably had it.

Then, I started reading the newspaper and learned there are several reports each winter about the debilitating effects of seasonal affective disorder. I become more depressed every time I read one of these.

A recent story from New York Times Syndicate quotes a staff member of the Canadian Mental Health Association as saying it took almost nine years before he was diagnosed with SAD. He remembers he could "go like (expletive deleted), get anything done" over the summer but "over the wintertimes I couldn't keep up that pace. It progressed downhill every year," he says.

That's me. I've been progressing downhill for at least 20 years. It's nice to know what's causing it.

The New York Times story says seasonal affective disorder was first noted before 1845 but wasn't officially recognized as a psychiatric diagnosis until the 1980's. There's no question a lot of folks were going downhill all of those years.

How does one know if they have seasonal affective disorder? A 1998 story from Knight Ridder/Tribune news service quotes one psychologist as saying, "It can be very dramatic — you can't think clearly at all. One person described it as feeling like his brain was encased in cold, 40-weight motor oil."

This patient was obviously a mechanic. How else would he know how a person's brain feels in 40-weight motor oil, as opposed to 30-weight or transmission fluid, for example?

The good news about SAD is that it can be treated with light therapy. The bad news is you have to buy some lights.

Those of us who get depressed at the price of lights can get some relief with a few common sense measures. Psychologists suggest we sit by a window at work or take a walk during the lunch hour.

People who work in their basement or some type of closet, as I do, might try sitting closer to their computer screen to soak up as much light as possible. News reporters can turn their cameras around and shoot the flash back into their faces occasionally.

Some do this several times a day, anyway. No one will notice you are doing it on purpose.

Folks who service cars and trucks should be careful to keep their heads out of the motor oil. Those who feel like their brain is encased in a stiff liquid might try standing in a hot shower for a few minutes. If that doesn't loosen things up, one of those electric dipstick heaters might help.

Above all, don't be afraid to do something others might consider stupid. It will cheer up your spouse if nothing else.

Tax Refund

Well it's about time. Congress and the President are finally going to do something about the IRS. We can be sure they won't do anything worthwhile, but at least they're going to do something.

Today I read the President and Congress want to give tax credits to companies that can reduce emissions of "greenhouse gases." A few days ago I noticed they want to increase tax credits for folks who need child care.

That's why we have the IRS. You can't give tax credits if you don't have a huge bureaucracy for collecting the greenbacks.

Proposals for improving the IRS include appointing citizens' committees that would get together and gripe on a regular basis, and/or abolish the agency — which would make taxes pretty much voluntary.

This summer I clipped a news report describing a metropolitan senator's speech to a group of farmers.

"I'd like to see a simple tax form," the Senator said. "Put your name at the top, write down all the income you had — perhaps with a few simple deductions — and at the end of the day send it off to the IRS."

How do you like that? All the income you had "perhaps with a few simple deductions" and send it off to the IRS?

Do they think we're stupid or what?! Why can't they just come by and take a cow and a few chickens like they used to?

The Senator went on to urge farmers to communicate with him about what they would like to see in a flat tax. I'll bet they communicated all right — soon after getting his attention with a flat piece of lumber.

I don't know what the answer is for this IRS hullabaloo, but I'm pretty sure a flat tax isn't it. Anybody who can list their income and deductions on a postcard doesn't have a paperwork problem in the first place.

Everyone has a favorite idea for dealing with federal tax collectors. Many folks like to pay more than they owe throughout the year and count on their yearly refund for paying bills and funding vacations.

This makes tax day a happy time when the taxpayer learns how much he will be getting back. It's a good way to save money if you don't have good control over yourself during the rest of the year.

I used to do the same thing when I raised a few pigs. I would go out in the spring and buy some pigs. Then I just kept buying feed and buying feed until the pigs got big enough to sell.

I always lost money on the deal. But I would take the money I got for the pigs and buy something I never could afford otherwise. The whole thing worked out great.

That's my approach to the IRS. I just toss them a check each morning and say, "Here you go boys. And don't you go and die on me before I get that refund back."

Order Form

Pine Forest Publishing
314 Pine Forest Road
Goldendale, WA 98620
Phone: 509-773-4718

Quantity	Item	Price	Total
	It's Hard To Look Cool When Your Car's Full Of Sheep (Humor)	$11.95	
	Things that go "Baa!" in the Night (Humor)	$11.95	
	My Dog Was A Redneck, But We Got Him Fixed (Humor)	$11.95	
	Take the Kids Fishing, They're Better Than Worms (Humor)	$11.95	
	Livestock Showman's Handbook (Informational)	$17.95	
	Book Total		
	Postage & Handling: $2.00 per book		
	Washington residents: Please add 7% sales tax		
	Grand Total		

Payment must accompany order.
Please make checks payable to *Pine Forest Publishing*.

Name _____

Address _____

City _____ State _____ Zip _____

Phone _____